A bad spin of the wheel at Cosmo's

"This is a perfectly respectable business deal, Studs." Ben Jolson kneed the door open and entered the dressing room.

Studs Gunny, the hottest shock-rock singer in the entire Barnum system, kicked a pair of lace-trimmed glopanties that lay crumpled on the floor near his chair. *"Muster* Gunny ter yer, yer shaggy hung of—"

"I'm on somewhat of a tight schedule." Shutting the door by shoving his wide gorilla backside against it, Jolson drew out his stungun.

"Ar, crikey! Anuffer looner attemptin' ter arsassinite me and—"

Zzzzzzzzzzummmmmmmm!

Holstering his gun, Jolson crossed to the chair and lifted the stunned shock-rock singer out of it. He tossed Gunny over his shoulder, turned and took five steps toward the closet he intended to store him in.

The closet door swung open; a lovely tanned hand holding a kilgun appeared. "I suspected that you were up to no good the moment I first saw you, Jolson."

The Exchameleon Series
by Ron Goulart
Published in paperback by St. Martin's Press

DAREDEVILS, LTD.

STARPIRATE'S BRAIN

EVERYBODY COMES TO COSMO'S

The Exchameleon Book 3

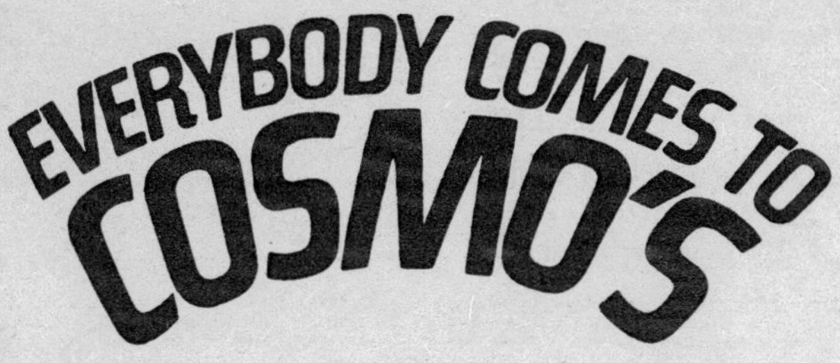

RON GOULART

ST. MARTIN'S PRESS/NEW YORK

EVERYBODY COMES TO COSMO'S

Library of Congress Catalog Card Number: 87-62616

ISBN: 0-312-90931-4 Can. ISBN: 0-312-90932-2

Printed in the United States of America

First St. Martin's Press mass market edition/February 1988

10 9 8 7 6 5 4 3 2 1

CHAPTER 1

He never got to complete that particular dinner.

The night was a clear, intense black. Beyond the glaz walls of the foyer of the tower restaurant the multicolored lights of the capital city of the largest territory on the planet Barnum gleamed and glittered like an infinity of gems. The thick thermocarpet was flecked with shimmering spots of silver and gold; the foyer, the lounge and the vast three-tiered dining room were crowded with handsomely dressed and well-groomed patrons.

Ben Jolson wished he were elsewhere.

He was standing in line and still two customers away from the headwaiter and the reservation book. Shifting his weight from one foot to the other, Jolson glanced toward the bar on his right.

Perched on a low pedestal was a pudgy catman in a tight-fitting purple tuxsuit. He was enthusiastically playing an electroviolin, eyes half shut in ecstasy, long orangish fur quivering.

"Look, Edmond, it's Merle and His Magic Violin,"

observed the husky lizard woman in line behind Jolson. "Isn't that exciting, seeing our favorite—"

"Shut your yap, Alma," suggested her tuxsuited green husband.

"Oh, come now," she said. "You're not going to let a silly little breakfast squabble spoil our evening on the town. Especially this unexpected bonus of hearing Merle and His Magic—"

"Making waffle marks all across my frapping backside with the microwaffler isn't my notion of a little squabble," responded Edmond. "Besides which, as any nitwit can plainly see, that's merely a Shobot sim of the actual Merle."

Frowning, his wife squinted at the adjacent cocktail lounge. "Are you sure, absolutely sure? What I mean is, Merle appears to be moderately tumescent, just as he was when we saw him in concert on—"

"Q-Mex Industries construct their Shobot androids that way, dimwit. They build them to be completely realistic replicas of show business greats, even down to getting fatons whilst serenading that crowd of affluent fatheads yonder in—"

"Yes?" The small yellowish toadman host was scrutinizing Jolson with an obvious lack of enjoyment.

The lean, lanky Jolson grinned bleakly. "Miss Briggs's table, please."

The toadman adjusted one of his blinking electric cuff links. "Surely, sir, you're not claiming that you're dining with Miss Briggs at EarthMom's this evening?" he inquired disdainfully.

"Matter of fact, I am."

"With Miss *Molly* Briggs?" He almost glanced at

the open reservation book on the stand near his sharp little left elbow.

"Yep, that's the one." Jolson leaned close to him. "As you no doubt are aware, Miss Briggs is a partner in the Briggs Interplanetary Detective Service. In her line of work it's only natural that she meets a great many lowlifes and criminals. Near saint that she is, she tries to rehabilitate a fallen felon now and then. I happen to be one such, sir, and I want to tell you that I'd still be known far and wide as the Phantom Toad Strangler had not that titian-haired little lady rescued me from the gutter and—"

"Phantom *what?*" asked the toadman.

"Toad Strangler. Naturally I didn't christen myself with that handle. It was the irresponsible media, who felt that simply because a fellow strangles a few toadmen he's fair game for their nasty—"

"Miss Briggs is in a private room on Tier 2, sir." The host smiled very briefly and took three steps back. "Follow the yellow gloline on the floor to that level, if you will."

"Thanks." Jolson followed the shimmering line into the immense dining room and then up a gently slanting ramp.

Molly Briggs was already in the plazwalled private room on the second level of EarthMom's. A slim, auburn-haired young woman, she was wearing a simple two-piece sinsilk frock. "I'm feeling more and more pleased about this evening," she said, smiling at him as he entered and sat opposite her at the small white table. "What I mean is, Ben, we really ought to get together like this more often. On a purely, entirely social basis. Sure, I am your employer at BIDS and you're bound to do my bidding by one of the toughest, most ironclad contracts in the entire Barnum System, but, heck, we're friends, too."

He eyed her. "I've fulfilled my obligation to your damn detective agency for the year," he reminded her. "That Starpirate case on Esmeralda last month satisfied my free-lance operative obligation to you and your father. Until next year, then, I intend to devote myself full time to my ceramics business and—"

"Actually, Ben, I do believe you and that clunky robot attorney of yours are reading your contract wrongly. I don't, by the way, see how you can trust in an attorney who only has two coats of enamel."

"I figured as much," said Jolson, nodding. "You lured me here tonight to try to stick me with another idiotic assignment for the Briggs Interplanetary Detective Service."

Her lovely hazel eyes went wide. "Golly, Ben, after all that you and I have been through together, you ought to trust me." Reaching out, she put a hand over his. "Honest, this is a social evening, pure and simple."

Jolson withdrew his hand from under hers. "You aren't going to talk business?"

"No, nope." She shook her head and her long hair brushed her bare shoulders. "Well, not any more than any two comrades in arms would, no." She coughed into her hand. "Well, how's ceramics?"

"Splendid."

"Are you still making those ugly little statuettes of . . . what are they called? Snergs?"

"The mania for snergs out in the Hellquad planets

has slackened some," he answered. "Right now, here on Barnum at any rate, ceramic kittens are very pop—"

"I hope, you know, you won't think I'm being nasty, Ben," she said. "But do you really consider what you do as being . . . well, artistic? What I'm getting at is, well, making dippy little statues of pussycats doesn't seem to be the sort of work a dedicated artist ought—"

"It's a business."

"So is being a private investigator for BIDS. And we pay a heck of a lot better." She drummed her fingertips on her menu. "If you were a full-time employee, the medical insurance and retirement benefits would be much better than—"

"I prefer ceramics as a way of life."

"But you're nearly fifty and—"

"Forty-two is not, technically, nearly fifty, Molly."

"Close enough. Anyway, I should think that a man who had been one of the crackerjack Chameleon Corps agents in the Barnum System for decades and decades would—"

"Twenty years. That's two decades."

"Ben, you have this really rare ability to change your shape, to assume all sorts of alternate identities at will," Molly said. "How can you let such a talent go to seed while you sit around and manufacture dinky little dornicks that—"

"Molly, I agreed to do a certain number of jobs per year for your agency," he cut in. "That more than satisfies my yen to do detective work and shapechanging. I'm an ex-Chameleon."

"So's my father, yet you don't see him sitting around on his duff while—"

"Hell, it's his agency. That gives him a different point of view."

"Another thing," she persisted. "If you worked full time for us, then you and I could work together on more assignments."

Jolson grinned and picked up his menu. "Ah, now we get to the romantic side of intergalactic investigation."

She snorted politely. "Don't go acting as though I'm trying to seduce you, Ben," she said. "I know, sure, that sometimes when we're out together on one of the wilder planets and I grow a bit overwrought . . . well, I have hugged and kissed you. Basically, though, ours is a brother-and-sister sort of relationship that—"

"Okay, sis, what say we order and shift to other topics?"

She wrinkled her faintly freckled nose. "I suggested EarthMom's because, even though they're fairly expensive, they serve Solar System style food and I was in the mood for some."

Jolson concentrated on his menu.

"Let me see now." Molly brought her menu up close to her face. "Grilled cheese sandwich. Am I ready for one of those? Side order of slaw. Nope, that doesn't sound quite appealing enough. How about ribs and grits? No, too spicy. Maybe I'll have the double cheeseburger. They offer fries and cola with it. Yes, that's what I'm—"

"Yikes!"

From down in the vicinity of the EarthMom's foyer someone, quite probably the host, had yelped. Rattlings, mutterings, exclamations of dismay came drifting up.

"Stop that dreadful little creature!"

"I got him, sir, and . . . Yow!"

"Gor and blimey, he up and froze Phillipe to the spot!"

Turning in his chair to face the doorway, Jolson reached his right hand into his jacket, toward the stungun in his shoulder holster.

The door of their private room whished open. "Jeez, if they allow bozos like Jolson in this dump, why make a fuss over my ankling up here?" A highly polished chrome-plated robot dog appeared on the threshold.

"Sniffer." Molly pushed back in her chair. "I thought I instructed you to remain at the BIDS offices until—"

"Spare me the sermon, Moll," Sniffer said. "We got us a problem. Even though I am more than capable of handling this latest mess solo, I thought it best to trot over here."

Molly said, "We can step outside and discuss whatever it—"

"Naw, we got to head out onto the highways and byways of this benighted burg right now quick."

"Why?"

"Because it looks like the client's nephew has gone off on a toot," the small robot hound informed her. "He's likely, therefore, to blab to all and sundry the nature of the assignment you have in mind for Beanpole Jolson and futz up our—"

"Client?" Jolson stood. "Assignment?"

"Oh, darn." Molly, sighing, got up and came around the table to take hold of Jolson's arm. "I really wasn't planning to tell you any of this until at least the dessert course."

CHAPTER 2

Jolson reached across Molly's lap, caught her hand and prevented her from turning on the engine of her skycar. "Before we go roaring off into the night," he said, "fill me in."

"Time's awastin'," muttered Sniffer from where he was sprawled in the backseat. "Young Quintillion is no doubt frying his conk in some low-down brainstim bistro even as you natter on about—"

"Is this strayed client part of the Quintillion clan?" asked Jolson. "That bunch on Murdstone who control Q-Mex and Shobots as well as—"

"Batsford Quintillion isn't our client exactly." Molly tapped her palms impatiently on her thighs. "He's the nephew of Janella Quintillion. She's the client, and he's the only relative she trusts enough to send here from their home planet to—"

"He's the *most* trustworthy, and he's a brainstim addict who—"

"She trusts him not to double-cross her in business matters," explained Molly. "That doesn't mean his moral outlook is—"

"This lad's run off to frequent the brainstim parlors here in the city?"

Sniffer said, "Boy, I knew I should've tackled this caper on my own, instead of letting you two ginzos procrastinate until—"

"I'm not procrastinating," said Molly, frowning back at the sprawled robot dog. "I'm more than ready to go and find the poor misguided boy and drag him back to the Ritz-Barnum Hotel, where we can get on with the business at—"

"Snif," asked Jolson, "how do you know he's running loose?"

"The rube pixphoned the agency to complain that he was growing bored and fretful in his suite. I took the call, and in my most persuasive and diplomatic manner informed him to park his toke right where it was until we got around to dropping in on him. Somehow young Batsford took offense, called me a 'tin-plated SOB' and vowed to go off and raise cain at the lowest brainstim establishment he could find."

"He's got a reputation for doing that sort of thing back home on Murdstone," added Molly. "I was assuming he'd reformed—at least for the duration of his stay on Barnum."

"A conversation with Sniffer could drive anybody out into the night."

"Can we perhaps blast off this goshdarn rooftop parking lot now?" implored the dog. "We're going to have to search every single brainstim—"

"Easier ways." Reaching out, Jolson punched a few buttons on the dash of the BIDS skycar.

Eleven seconds elapsed, then a small faxprint photo of Batsford Quintillion came easing out of a silver-rimmed slot. He was a pudgy, bland-faced young man of about twenty-five with frizzy yellow hair.

"Hardly worth hunting for," commented Jolson as he punched out a number on the dial below the pixphone screen.

"Let's get airborne," grumbled the robot dog.

"Hush," advised Molly, watching Jolson.

On the screen appeared a fat, green-feathered birdman in a three-piece sky-blue glosuit. He was leaning back in a padded desk chair, his booted feet up on a cluttered ivory desk. His orange beak was clicking in time with the music of an unseen violin and he was snapping his feathery fingers. "High class, huh, Ben?" he said.

"Which?"

"I just got me a Merle and His Magic Violin Shobot to play here at my Shadowland Slim's Topless Bird Babe Bar and Grill," explained Shadowland Slim. "It's high class, ain't it?"

"Sounds like." He held up the picture of Batsford Quintillion to the pixphone eye. "I'm interested in locating this fellow, Slim. He's a brainstim buff and ought to be, I figure, either in Underbelly 16 or Underbelly 17 about now."

Shadowland Slim nodded. "Give me around ten minutes, Ben, and I'll find out which sector and what dump. Where can I pix you?"

Giving him the car number, Jolson clicked off. "This ought to be simpler than—"

"Depending on informants and stoolies," commented Sniffer, "is not my idea of deduction at its finest."

Jolson rolled up the photo of Quintillion. "Okay,

Molly, what sort of case are you trying to involve me in?"

"Oh, forget it." She slumped in the driveseat. "What I mean is, here I was trying to con you and behaving in a shameful and shameless manner. Trading on your honest affection for me, attempting to vamp you into taking a job." She shook her head forlornly. "However can you put up with such brazen—"

"Q-Mex is on the *Galactic Fortune* list of the top five hundred companies." He unfurled the picture and studied the dull face. "They're obviously paying BIDS a large—larger than usual—fee."

"Sort of, yes," admitted Molly.

"Meaning that you and your pop can well afford to offer me a bonus on this one." He rubbed the faxprint across his chin. "A bonus big enough to allow me to buy that new kiln I need for my ceramics business. Say, fifty thousand trubux."

"No more than twenty-five," Molly said, sitting up straight. "Besides, I'm wondering if we ought to offer this one to one of our other ex-Chameleon operatives, one who's a shade more enthusiastic. After all, out in the field it's the spirit and—"

The pixphone buzzed, interrupting her sentence and Jolson's responsive laughter.

He answered the call.

Shadowland Slim appeared once again. "The chump you seek, Ben, is right now at Shock Gibson's club."

"Much obliged, Slim."

"Think nothing of it. This simply puts you even more in my eternal debt." The screen blanked.

Jolson turned to Molly. "Forty thousand."

"Thirty."

"A deal," he said, grinning. "Now fly us over to the Underbelly 16 sector."

Sighing quietly, she started the skycar. "I keep forgetting how mercenary you are," she said. "And to think that while I was in college I used to look up to you as a man of sterling integrity."

"Which proves you should never trust a schoolgirl's judgment," he told her. "While we're flying over there you can give me more background stuff on this case."

The skycar throbbed, went zooming off the rooftop parking area and up into the glittering night.

After setting the skycar on an automatic flypattern for the outskirts of the capital, Molly said, "I don't have all the details on the case as yet. Janella Quintillion is, as you know, the president and chairman of the board of Quintillion Mechanix, better known as Q-Mex throughout the universe. They net untold billions of trudollars each and every year from Shobots, the most successful show-biz andies on the market. And they also manufacture a whole stewpot of other gadgets and mechanisms."

"They may be smart," Sniffer interjected, "yet they never got around to coming out with a robot sleuth hound that's anywhere near as clever as—"

"Janella Quintillion is apparently the only surviving child of the late Amoz Quintillion, founder of the whole shebang," continued Molly as the skycar whizzed across the night city.

"Why *apparently* the only survivor?"

"She had an older brother and sister, but they're dead and gone."

"Really defunct or only presumed so?"

Molly toyed with a strand of her auburn hair. "Oh, both of them are dead and done for," she said. "But when I was chatting with our client via scrambled sat/pix phone call yesterday—well, she seemed to be hinting that there's a missing heiress involved in this someplace."

"Is that what she wants BIDS to do, find a lost relative?"

"Right now we just have to get an op out to the planet Murdstone. Janella Quintillion will fill you in on the rest of what she wants when you get there, Ben."

"What about this wandering nephew?"

"Our client apparently doesn't want her other relatives—most of whom hold positions in Q-Mex—to know she's hiring us. She doesn't trust them," explained Molly. "Batsford, bless his frazzled brain, is the only one of her myriad kin she more or less trusts. So—"

"I impersonate him and go home in his place."

Nodding, she said, "Exactly, yes. That gets you safely into Q-Mex and our client's mansion without anybody catching on. You pop in on her, get all the details and then contact me."

"You're planning to come to Murdstone, too?"

"Gosh, you don't have to sound so downcast at the prospect of teaming up with me again."

Jolson tipped a thumb in the direction of the sprawled robot dog. "You, I can tolerate. It's your sidekick who causes me severe abdominal cramps, jittery nerves and severe heebie-jeebies."

"Well, I probably won't be taking him along if I do

decide, after I get your report from the field, that the case is serious enough to—"

"Good thing, folks, I am chrome-plated," put in Sniffer. "Otherwise these cruel barbs would sink right into my loyal little heart. If you really have the brains I give you credit for, Moll, you'll dump slim-jim here and embark for picturesque Murdstone, pearl of the universe, with just me and my built-in array of first-rate forensic—"

"Be still or it's into the trunk with you," warned the young woman. "Actually, Ben, I don't intend to travel to Murdstone with you when you take off tomorrow morning from the spaceport. I won't come out there at all unless the case is really important."

"Let's hope that it is," he said.

CHAPTER 3

In one of the murky alleys off the main street of Underbelly 16 somebody was broiling a dog. The mingled smells of cooking flesh, sizzling lard and strong spices came spilling out at Jolson as he made his way to Shock Gibson's brainstim parlor.

He was alone and on foot, moving rapidly along the rutted sidewalk and running an obstacle course composed of derelicts, garbage, offal and excrement.

"Here now, that front paw's mine," complained a husky voice from within the alley.

"Like bloody blazes it is, cobber. Mine is whose it is."

"Mine, because I contributed the blooming recipe from *Galactic Gourmet* for the making of fricasseed terrier, didn't I? Therefore, by all that's—"

"A lot you know about haute cuisine. This ain't a terrier, it's a ruddy cocker spaniel, and . . ."

Jolson hopped over the torso of a fallen android.

"Mate," requested the dented head of the andy, "would yer do a bloke a perishing favor and fetch me my legs from that there ash can yonder? A pack of wicked urchins unfastened me pins and left me—"

"Still using the missing-legs dodge, Gaspar?"

"Ar, it's you, Jolson. Excuse it, pal, I didn't recognize you on account of me plaz eyes are in need of replacement and—"

"Not a trupenny." Jolson continued on his way.

He passed the Derring-Do Deli— "The Most Violent Dining Spot on the Entire Planet!" *Galactic Gourmet* was quoted as proclaiming in a glosign over the arched doorway—just as two husky lizardmen dockwallopers were tossed out through the front window along with a plazplate containing a thin wedge of blueberry cheesecake.

"Complain about the size of the portions, will you?" roared a copper-plated robot bouncer, wiping his big hands on his apron. "We'll show you who's generous and who ain't."

The green stevedores, the inadequate slice of cheesecake and hundreds of tinkling fragments of window glaz hit the cracked pavement a few feet ahead of Jolson. Dodging into the gutter, nearly stepping on a sleeping orphan, he hurried on.

He went by Swill's Cafe, the Green Supremacy Party headquarters, the Fifty Fat Ladies Fastsex Bordello, the Murder Inc. Donut Shop and the Club of Queer Trades.

The glosign over the narrow entryway to Shock Gibson's was on the fritz and was sputtering, dying, blinking back to brief life.

An apeman doorman was mounted on a shaky stool, whapping at the sign with a neowood mallet. "C'mon, sweetie pie. Work, work for papa. C'mon, illuminate, damn it."

Whap! Whap!

Edging around the teetering stool, Jolson descended the five sudostone steps to the scarlet door.

He entered the brainstim establishment, halted on the yellow glofloor and glanced around. The room was long and narrow, with rows of numbered doors on each side.

A teenage birdgirl, clad in a two-piece sinsilk pajama suit, was perched on a padded stool to the right of the entrance and had a battered tin money box on one knee. "Welcome to Shock Gibson's, sir. What's your pleasure for this evening?" she began reciting. "Euphoria? Hallucinations? Orgasm? Brainfry? Simulated death? Shock Gibson's offers you ninety-nine—that's correct, you heard right. Shock Gibson's offers ninety-nine different kinds of brainstim, each and every one utilizing the most advance brainstim machines available anywhere in the Barnum System of planets. And yes, all at the low, low prices for which Shock—"

"Which room's this gent in?" He showed her the picture of the strayed Batsford Quintillion.

She blinked, scowled. "Here now, you ought not to interrupt me in midspiel like that," she complained. "Now I got to go all the way back to the very start, since I learned this by rote. Welcome to Shock Gibson's, sir. What's your—"

"Actually, I'm not a customer."

Her orange feathers fluttered on her head. "What are you, then? A flatfoot? A narco? An electro? A bunco? A—"

"Well, I happen to be this fellow's nurse at the Horrible Disease Hospice over in Restricted Zone 6," he explained with an amiable grin. "He has a tendency to go over the wall, run amok for a while and then head for places like—"

"Horrible disease, did you say?"

Nodding, Jolson said, "To ensure the safety and well-being of all concerned, the sooner I get him back to the total isolation ward and locked away in his germproof—"

"Is it contagious?"

Tilting his head to one side, Jolson was studying the teen birdgirl. "Hum?"

"I said, is this dink's disease something people could catch? Something I myself might . . . What are you giving me the once-over for?"

"Oh, I'm probably wrong."

"Wrong about what?"

He let out a sad sigh. "This unfortunate young man happens to be suffering from the pip," he explained, backing a few paces from the girl. "We've found that birdpeople are especially susceptible to the pip. But . . . well, your symptoms could just as easily be caused by some other ailment that isn't at all life-threatening or fatal in any—"

"What symptoms?"

"Eh?" He cupped his hand to his ear.

"What symptoms do you mean, Doctor?"

"Ah, that's a pity. You're obviously trying to talk, yet no sound is coming out," he said, shaking his head forlornly. "That is one of the signs that the victim is suffer—"

"I can hear myself. Are you certain that—"

"If you can tell me where my patient is, miss, then I can whisk him away from here before this spreads to any of the others."

"Room 14." She pointed a feathered finger at a door across the room.

"Say, I heard you that time," he said. "Perhaps you aren't as bad off as you look." He started toward the door she'd indicated.

"What should I do, Doctor?"

"Head for home, pop in bed, rest for a full day at least."

"Am I going to pass away?"

"No, no, you needn't worry about that eventuality, young lady. Why, there's really only a 95 percent chance that it'll be fatal in your particular case, so—"

"Ninety-five percent? But there's only a 100 percent altogether, so if I have 95 percent—"

"Go get plenty of rest," he advised and opened the door to Room 14.

Batsford Quintillion fell down again. "Go on without me, sport," he mumbled, settling into a flat-out position on the dingy cobblestones of the alley behind Shock Gibson's place of business.

Bending, Jolson took hold of the partially stupefied young man under the armpits and yanked him to a kneeling position. Then, using one of Quintillion's arms as a lever, he got him upright.

"Ah, you have a gentle touch, sport. Much like old Nanny Botz, that sweet, loyal old family nursebot who raised generations of—"

"Commence walking," advised Jolson.

"Good old Nanny Botz." Tears appeared at the corners of the pudgy young man's small pale blue eyes. "I hurt her with my wicked, wicked ways, Johnson . . . That is your name, isn't it, old cock? I haven't lived up to the simple faith that sweet maternal mechanism placed in me when I was a wee lad. Oh, the folly of it all." He slumped against Jolson's chest and began sobbing.

Jolson tossed him over his shoulder and started walking.

"Where is that beloved 'bot today? Put out to pasture like the snows of yesteryear," mumbled Quintillion, still far from recovered from his encounter with the brainstim machine in Room 14.

Jolson carried the client's nephew along a narrow street that led back to where the BIDS skycar waited.

Quintillion said, "All women aren't as loyal as Nanny Botz, let me tell you, Jessup. Ah, no. Are you married?"

Jolson made no reply.

"Betty Lou is not at all like Nanny Botz. Not at all, old cock. That's where flesh and blood lets one down. Better let Q-Mex build you a wife than trust a . . . Poor old Nanny. Packed away in the lumber room of the past. Served Aunt Janella and the rest of them, too. Generations of Q-Mex execs knew and loved . . . You know, Betty Lou's a damn silly name for a woman. It'd even be a silly name for a pet snerg, now I think of it. Betty Lou. Did ever a poet pen a poem in praise of a Betty Lou? Do poets even use pens anymore? What's your opinion, Johansen? We'd like to know, and we'll give the best replies to our editorial equal time. Betty Lou. I rue the day I . . ." He ceased muttering, began snoring.

A half block short of the skycar a wheelbot cop came rolling out of an alley and directly into Jolson's path. The blue enameled cop aimed a gun hand at him. "Halt, sir or madam."

Jolson obliged.

"Are you," inquired the lawbot, "carrying that chap off for any criminal purpose?"

"Nope."

"Okay, good. Because I'm built to prevent crime." The robot rolled on by him. "Have a nice evening."

As he approached the skycar, which was parked on the pavement near a corner, the rear door popped open.

"Holy cow, did you go and bump off our client's kinsman before we've even collected our fee?" Sniffer poked his plaz nose out into the night.

"He only sleeps." Jolson deposited the unconscious Quintillion across the rear seat.

"Have any trouble?" asked Molly as Jolson slid into the passenger seat next to her.

"Not much, no." He strapped on his safety gear. "But you're going to have to pay me thirty-five thousand for this job."

"Why?"

"The extra five thousand is to compensate me for having to impersonate Batsford," he answered.

CHAPTER 4

Molly's parlor seemed to be the living room of a rustic lodge. The walls appeared to be of rough-hewn realwood, the ceiling was beamed. A log fire was apparently blazing in a deep stone fireplace, and peaceful night woodlands showed outside the windows.

"You can sit," suggested Molly, "on that comfortable leather sofa."

Jolson tried that, fell clear through the tri-op projection and thumped the floor with his backside. "Very droll," he observed, rising.

"Darn! I wasn't trying to play a dumb joke on you," she told him. "There's supposed to be a real sofa right under that image. It really, you know, annoys me when I pay thirty-four thousand trubux for this new Enviroscope System to liven up my parlor, plus shell out two hundred and sixty an hour to each of the goons who installed it, and then have you sit on air."

He held his palms toward the illusory fire. "Maybe we can withdraw to another room so you can finish briefing me on what I'm supposed to do on this Quintillion case."

"That'd be giving up." She was frowning, scanning

the room. "Very carefully, Ben, poke that apparent rustic chair directly under the stuffed grout head on the wall. There's supposed to be a real chair lurking within that tri-op projection."

Grinning, he poked. "Desk, feels like."

"Okay, all right. We'll use the kitchen, if you don't mind."

"Not at all."

Molly scanned the room again, then starting moving. "There ought to be a real door right about here," she said, grabbing at an apparent doorknob. "Yes, it is." She yanked it open.

As he followed her along the corridor a restless thumping started in the closet on his left.

"Help, help, whoever you are. Rescue me from this foul prison."

Molly gave the closet door a kick. "Be still, Sniffer," she cautioned. "I warned you you'd end up in there if you didn't stop razzing Ben."

"There isn't any reading material in here," complained the robot dog. "Also I like to pace at this time of the evening, which is nigh on to impossible in this cramped little—"

"You hush up and behave, and I'll let you out as soon as Ben goes."

"How cruel, that you'd toss me into this makeshift pokey simply so that you can schmooze with that lank—"

"Enough," she said, continuing on her way to the kitchen.

Molly watched him set his teacup back on the kitchen table, amidst the scatter of briefing materials spread out there. "Well, it's supposed to taste sort of metallic," she said. "What I mean is, peppermint tea always has a strong metallic taste."

"Tonight anyway."

"I'm certain this new tea-brewing unit I just bought can't be fouling up. After all, you pay fourteen hundred and sixty trubux for a dinky little tea-brewing unit and it's obviously got to work like a dream." She sipped her tea. "Yes, that tastes fine. Peppermint is supposed to taste very much like metal filings. I'm surprised you didn't realize that right off."

He said, "We got Batsford Quintillion stowed away at the Renfrew Brothers Detox Country Club. And I'm supposed to be him for the—"

"Those Renfrews better be able to fix him up quick —I don't know, though, I somehow find it hard to put my faith in twins who don't even look alike—because Batsford, the real Batsford, has to be home on Murdstone by early next week."

"Is that tied in with this case?" He leaned both elbows on the white tabletop.

"No, it's a very important Q-Mex business meeting. Batsford has to be there in person—no sat projections allowed. There're papers to be signed and so on."

"I'll arrive on Murdstone two days hence, see our client and find out exactly what she wants," he said. "By the time Batsford gets home I'll have no further use for his identity."

"Probably not." She tried another very brief sip of her tea.

"You don't know anything else about the assignment?"

"Only that it's very important and probably dangerous."

"Batsford was mentioning his wife," said Jolson. "I got the impression that they were not the most idyllic couple in—"

"According to the somewhat cursory report sent me by a field op out there, she's a . . ." Molly rummaged through the memos, printouts and faxpages she'd dumped on the table between them. She located a photo. "This is she—somewhat too ample in the chest to my way of thinking, but pretty, I suppose. Twenty-six years old, blonde at the moment. Went to school in the Earth System of planets and graduated—barely—from the Mars campus of the University of California."

"Attractive," he decided after studying the picture. "Probably mean, though, judging by the eyes and the mouth."

"Supposedly she . . . um . . . well, she hasn't exactly been completely faithful to Batsford during the three years of their marriage," said Molly. "Although perhaps you can't be faithful to a man with a name like Batsford."

"How does he react to all this?"

"To what, to being cuckolded?"

"I'm going to be impersonating the guy. I have to know whether he broods about her fooling around, smacks her, or goes and complains to his chums."

"Oh, yes, sure." She picked up a sheet of yellow faxpaper. "Here's some background on that aspect of their relationship. You probably aren't going to get anywhere near Betty Lou Quintillion anyway." She passed across the report, eyes on his face. "When you do one of these impersonations . . . What I mean is, if you're supposed to be somebody's husband . . . um . . . would you . . . ?"

"Sure."

"Oh." She picked up her cup, sipped again. "Funny, I always thought I liked peppermint."

CHAPTER 5

The super-first-class passengers cocktail lounge on the S.S. *Swiftwing* was not crowded. The mighty spaceliner had just made its hyperspace jump and many of the Murdstone-bound passengers were recovering from that in their cabins.

Jolson was now, thanks to the abilities built into him by the rigorous and complex Chameleon Corps processing years ago, an exact replica of the recuperating Batsford Quintillion. Pudgy, pale-eyed and rather dull-looking, he sat alone at a table near the small floating circular stage.

A chimpman in a too-large three-piece flashing silver tuxsuit had just hopped onto the stage. Standing on tiptoe to reach the dangling mike, he announced to the fewer than a dozen customers scattered around the blank-walled room, "Now, folks, it's my pleasure to introduce three sexy singing simulacra. Yessir, it's the universally loved and respected Angerbanger Sisters—Mitzi, Fritzi and Ritzi. And here they come to belt out for you their latest interplanetary hit, 'The Boogie-Woogie Rocket Jockey.' "

"Say there, sport," called out Jolson in his nasal

Batsford Quintillion voice. "Aren't you forgetting a little something?"

The furry MC was about to jump from the stage to the ebony lounge floor. "No heckling, chum."

Three lovely green-skinned androids were climbing the short ramp to the stage.

"Read your contract again, old cock," advised Jolson, a nasty edge slipping into his voice. "I do believe you'll find it clearly states that at no time are you to introduce these impressive mechanisms without using the standard phrase: 'These are genuine Shobots, manufactured by Quintillion Mechanix.' "

The chimpman shrugged. "So once in a while I forget, bud. Ain't important."

"Get your shaggy butt back up there and say it, friend," ordered Jolson. "Or I'll have you severed from your job."

"Who the fudd do you—"

"My name happens to be Batsford Quintillion. I'd hate to have to summon Captain DeFuccio, yet I assure you that—"

"Quintillion, did you say?"

Smirking, Jolson merely nodded.

The MC scuttled to a position under the mike. "Folks, I got to tell you, these are genuine Shobots, manufactured by Quintillion Mechanix." Hunching his shoulders, he dropped the four feet from the stage to the floor. Without looking again at Jolson he headed for an exit.

Mitzi, Fritzi and Ritzi Angerbanger went into their song.

A slim rainbow-haired young woman came over to stand next to his table. "You're sure him, all right."

"Go away," he suggested. "I don't wish to be hustled by any floozies this evening."

"Quit being a dunk. I'm with the press." Uninvited, she sat opposite him. "Yep, you're as futzy as they told me you'd be. Well, there's no avoiding it. I got to get a hundred and fifty words out of you, Quintillion."

"On the contrary, young lady, you'll get a swift—"

"Listen, you have to go along with this. Q-Mex never turns down a chance for free publicity." From her large neowicker purse the thin reporter extracted a talking business card. "This'll expl—"

"INTRODUCING MISS TIMMY TEMPEST," boomed the voxcard she was holding out to Jolson, "REPORTER AT LARGE FOR *GALACTIC VARIETY!*"

Noticing that he was reluctant to take the card, Timmy said, "It doesn't overheat anymore, not since I had it overhauled on . . . But how the heck did you know that my bizcard used to—"

"Miss Tempest, I make it a practice not to accept any unsolicited business cards."

"INTRODUCING MISS TIMMY—" repeated the card in its loud, rich voice.

She shut it back up in her purse, cutting off its message. "Now that we know each other, let's get down to business," Timmy said, leaning toward him. "Lucky I bumped into you like this, because you're one of the ginks I was assigned to look up once I got to your dumpy home planet. I got a whole uninspiring list of uninspiring people to—"

"Go away."

"C'mon, don't be a dumpus, Q. All I need from you is a short, halfway intelligent comment on this latest

Shobot of yours. The one that's just sold a hundred thousand copies across the universe, making it the top—"

"You can say that Q-Mex is gratified, as always, that one of its superior android entertainers has succeeded in capturing the public fancy. Now scram."

Timmy scowled. "What kind of dippy answer is that? Sounds like the usual PR crapola to me," she informed him. "Naw, the real angle here is that this Shobot is based on Studs Gunny, the hottest shock-rock singer in the entire Barnum System. Everybody knows that the real Studs Gunny has been dorking your missus on the sly. How's that hit you, Q?"

"Go away, begone."

"I see it as sort of the classic conflict," she continued. "Mammon versus love. Should you cancel the Studs Gunny Shobots and bid your spouse to have nothing more to do with the gunk? Or are the prospects of so much dough pouring in so overwhelming that you just keep quiet about what's going on? Or did you maybe sic your sexy better half on Studs Gunny in the first place to persuade him to sign with Q-Mex and not your dread rival, Interplanet Robot and Android? The possibilities are almost infinite!"

"I advise you, Miss Tempest, to go off at once and contemplate them," he told her. "Keeping in mind that the laws of libel and slander in our planet system tend to favor the person who is libeled and not the mean-minded media simp who maligns him."

Timmy said, "Another thing that's fascinating, Q, is the fact that Studs Gunny is an albino toadman. How do you feel about your wife hopping between the old sheets with a toad? Seems to me it's bad enough to have your mate shtupping with one of your own kind, but a toad. A colorless toad with close-together little pinky eyes. Unk."

Slumping in his chair, Jolson brought both hands up to his pudgy, puffy face. "Cruel," he murmured, commencing to cry. "How cruel the press is when a man is in distress." He let his head drift down until it was resting on the tabletop.

"Glory, what a maudlin dunk you can be at times." She stood, clutching her purse to her narrow chest. "I believe I will go to my cabin. I can just fake this particular yarn."

Jolson continued to sob until the rainbow-haired young woman was gone from the cocktail lounge.

CHAPTER 6

The afternoon wind threw great swirls of snow against the dome that sheltered the Murdstone Spaceport 7 landcar parking area.

"Bit of a rum day, eh, sir?" observed the medium-sized valebot struggling toward the waiting Q-Mex landlimo weighted down with six of Jolson's suitcases. "Not as bad as last week's blizzard, however, which you fortunately missed."

"Perhaps, Jorrocks, it's time for you to revisit the Shop."

The servo slowed, plump pinkish face paling, fine-spun white hair fluttering. "Oh, I think not, sir. Lord, it was only just two years ago that I went in for a complete overhaul and—"

"You've been babbling far too much of late, old cock."

"Far be it from me to disagree with you, sir, since it's not my place to do so," said Jorrocks. "I do hope, though, that you will allow me to point out that the Q-Mex Benign Old Servitor/Model 30F, of which I am a prime example, was designed to blather and dodder a bit. That's the traditional style for—"

"Best learn to curb the prattle, sport, or it's in for another overhaul," warned Jolson. "Stow my baggage now, if you would, and we'll get rolling."

The android halted at the rear of the silvery landlimo. "Ups-a-daisy," he said, and the trunk popped open. "I trust, sir, you had a pleasant time on Barnum."

"Pleasant enough."

After getting the last of the realeather suitcases stacked neatly in the trunk, Jorrocks came shuffling around to the side of the vehicle. "Open, please."

The door to the rear compartment swung silently open. Jolson, with the valebot assisting, climbed in and settled on the wide realeather seat. "Let's get out of here, Jorrocks."

"To be sure, sir." The mechanical servant hurried to the other side of the landlimo, opened the door and slid in behind the controls.

Settling back further, Jolson told Jorrocks, "I want to go to Aunt Jan's first."

The large vehicle rolled from the plazdomed lot into the roadway. The snow hit at them, whirling all around. There was little traffic and the streets were a slick black spotted with white.

Brrrttttzzzz! Brrtttzzzz!

Jolson sighed, leaned forward and clicked on the pixphone screen that was mounted in the back of the front seat. "What is it?"

A plump green woman of forty appeared on the small rectangular screen. "Welcome home, Mr. Quintillion," she said, smiling carefully and brushing at her bright purple hair. "Everyone at Quintillion Mechanix is delighted that you've returned safely from—"

"Erna, whatever is that atop your head?"

"My hair, Mr. Quintillion." She was seated behind a black rubberoid desk that had several neat stacks of faxpapers and memos atop it. "At what time may we expect you here at the office? I have several—"

"Your hair didn't used to be purple, old girl."

"So thoughtful of you to notice. I decided to perk up my image a bit by—"

"Tomorrow, no later," he informed Batsford Quintillion's private secretary, "your hair will be its usual drab orange."

She patted the hair again. "Are you implying that—"

"I should've thought you'd realize I don't want a secretary with purple hair," he said. "Reflect on that, Erna, and decide whether it's to be you or the hair that leaves Q-Mex. I'll be there quite late this afternoon, if at all." He broke the connection. "Fool woman."

"No accounting for vanity, sir."

"Are you also programmed to mouth dim-witted platitudes?"

"Afraid so, sir."

"Strive to control that impulse." He settled back, closing his eyes.

Brrrtttzzz! Brrrrttttzzzz!

"This is turning into a very vexing homecoming." He turned on the pixphone. "Now what?"

"Watch your tone when you're chatting with me, butthole," advised the tanned, handsome man who showed up on the phonescreen. "This isn't one of your flunkies."

"Excuse me, Cousin Destry," said Jolson, sitting

up. "I had a rather stressful jaunt out from Barnum, which accounts for—"

"Quit brownnosing, bunghole. Be in my office here at four."

"Really, Destry, I don't think I can—"

"Bats, this isn't a debate we're in the midst of, fella," Destry Quintillion told him. "We're having a small problem with the Studs Gunny subrights. Since that bimbo you're married to is—"

"Damn it, Destry, I'm having enough trouble with Betty Lou without your suggesting we have her sweet-talk that toad into—"

"Four o'clock. No excuses." The screen went blank.

"Not a very pleasant person, if I may say so, sir."

"It's a family trait."

Brrrrttttzzzz! Brrrrtttzzz!

"Yes?"

An obese catman in a rumpled two-piece bizsuit was on the screen.

Jolson had absolutely no idea who this seedy catman was. "Hold on a sec, old cock." He blanked his side of the conversation. "Jorrocks, old man, that hyperspace jump seems to have addled my memory a mite. Do you recognize this fellow's voice?"

"Sounds very much like the uncouth tones of Bullet Benton, sir."

"And who is he?"

Making a throat-clearing sound, Jorrocks said, "One hesitates to bring up what may be a delicate—"

"Quick, who the hell is Bullet Benton?"

"He is, sir, the private inquiry agent whom you hired last month to keep tabs, as it were, on your errant wife. I must say any chap who'd call his business the Acme Detective Agency evinces a certain lack of imagin—"

"That's sufficient." He turned his end of things back on. "Anything new for me, Benton?"

"Wellsir, if you're certain this is a good time to talk," said the furry detective, "I shall get under way with my latest report. First off, I'll read you the newest list of the gentlemen with which your little lady's been unfaithful. For convenience's sake I've put their handles down alphabetically. After that, I'll play you a sampling of the vidtaped and sonibugged transcriptions of the various—"

"Is this likely, Benton, to be a lengthy report?"

"Wellnow, Mr. Q, they usually are, aren't they?" The catman fished a wad of faxpaper from an inner pocket of his wrinkled green jacket. "Let's just see how many there are this time around. Five . . . eight . . . ten . . . Nope, that's the same fellow repeating. Now it's ten . . . fourteen . . . Although maybe—"

"I'm short on time just now," cut in Jolson. "Try me at my office first thing in the morning, will you?"

"The list may grow a bit more by—"

"Nevertheless." He ended the call, sat back again and gazed out at the heavily falling snow.

"May one offer one's sympathy, sir?"

"One may as well."

Jolson stepped into the blind corridor and left the light and sound of the afternoon behind. The petite android maid moved soundlessly along the dark brown hall; the thick brown thermocarpet swallowed Jolson's footfalls as well.

The corridor curved, twisted and ended.

The dark-haired maid stood aside, gesturing at an opaque forcescreen door. When Jolson touched the door, it shimmered, made a faint harp-twang sound and vanished.

The huge living room beyond had plaz walls of a blackish-brown shade. All the furniture was in dark earth colors and the only light came from strips of illumination that circled the room at floor level.

A gaunt, gray-haired woman in her late fifties sat stiffly in a dark brown armchair.

Bending over her, holding her wrist, was a tall, lean frogman in a three-piece gray bizsuit. He turned slowly, blinking at Jolson. "I'm gravely concerned, Batsford," he said in a low, mournful voice.

"Just as I am, Dr. Salt." He crossed the threshold and the door formed again behind him. "I wish I could say you were looking better, Aunt Jan."

Janella Quintillion said, "If you two worrywarts would stop trying to convince me I'm ready for the grave, I really think I'd start to improve. I sometimes think I'm simply the victim of your negative propaganda."

"She's lost nearly three more pounds," said the green doctor, straightening and moving away from her. "If this keeps up, Janella, you'll—"

"Yes, yes, I know."

As he passed Jolson, Dr. Salt said, "There's little hope, my boy."

When the doctor was gone, Janella said, "My biggest mistake has been to surround myself with idiots. Now then, let's get—"

"Not right yet, Aunt Jan." From a trouser pocket Jolson took a small bug detector. He began a slow circuit of the room, holding the gadget in the palm of his hand. "Never talk business unless you're sure you're bugfree. You taught me that."

"All the rooms in the mansion are gone through at dawn each day, Jolson, so it's—"

"What an odd thing to call me, Aunt Jan. Though I guess it's better than Bats, which is—"

"This counterespionage routine doesn't impr—"

"Patience, Auntie." Satisfied that the living room was free of eavesdropping devices, he put away the small detector and sat on a dark brown sofa chair facing their client. "I don't put on shows for the customers, Miss Quintillion. Don't, please, go blurting out my name before we're sure the—"

"Yes, yes, I'm sorry." She waved away his rebuke with a thin, knobby hand. "Do you, by the way, want a few tips on how to improve your impersonation of my nephew?"

He grinned. "Sure."

"You weren't arrogant enough with the doctor," she said. "You ought to slouch a bit more, and try to appear a good deal more bleary-eyed."

"This better?" He slouched in the chair, modified his puffy face.

"Yes," she said, adding, "very impressive."

"Were you aware that Batsford had hired a detective of his own—or at least a moderate facsimile of a detective?"

"Yes, to keep an eye on Betty Lou," she replied. "All that has, I assure you, nothing to do with my summoning a Briggs Interplanetary Detective Service operative here."

"I'd prefer not to have dicks like Bullet Benton underfoot."

"When Batsford comes home, I'll persuade him to fire the man," she promised, smiling faintly. "One doesn't, after all, need a detective to confirm that girl's infidelity."

Jolson studied the brown ceiling for a few seconds. "He's your favorite, huh? Batsford is?"

"You haven't met the others, Jolson."

"Had a brief phone conversation with Destry."

"The worst of the lot. Well, actually there's some competition for that title."

"Okay, what do you want BIDS to do for you?"

She folded her thin, faintly blue hands in her narrow lap. "Find my sister."

"Then those old rumors are true?"

Janella said, "I take it you've researched my background and that of my family."

"We do that routinely on most clients. At least the ones who pay fees the size of yours."

"It's probably fitting, since I'm the head of such an organization as Quintillion Mechanix, that I myself am—in a way—the result of a technological process," she said. "My father, Amoz Quintillion, founded Q-Mex. I never, of course, knew him or my mother. Two years before I was born, they were both killed in the destruction of a spaceliner bound for Esmeralda."

"But they'd left two lab-conceived embryos behind at a place in the next territory known as the Seagate Clinic," he said.

She nodded. "My brother and other sister were small children then, yet there was considerable legal skirmishing set off by our relatives," she said. "That delayed things, so the embryo wasn't implanted in a surrogate mother for well over a year. But by the time they went to get the other one—another girl, let me mention, since my parents had no prejudice against having females eventually run Quintillion Mechanix—it was gone."

"Stolen?"

"They initially believed it was taken from the Seagate Clinic as part of a kidnap scheme. Yet no ransom demands were ever made."

"Did the family try to trace it?"

"Some effort was made at the time, yes," she said. "None of them, keep in mind, was all that anxious to have yet another Quintillion heiress. I was bad enough." Janella made a faint, sad sound that was meant to be laughter. "I survived, I outlasted all of that generation. Now, as you can see, Jolson, I'm dying."

"You're certain?"

"As certain as I need to be, yes."

"You refer to a lost sister, but you have no proof at all that that embryo was ever allowed to become a child."

"None at all, no," she admitted. "There are, however, several possibilities I wish to have explored. If the child was born, where is she now? Is she the same age as I am? Perhaps that embryo wasn't implanted until forty years ago, or thirty or twenty. Or possibly it was never implanted, yet still exists and is viable. There is also the possibility it was long ago destroyed. Whatever the answer, Jolson, I have to know. My sister, if she lives, is heiress to all of this, everything." She made the forlorn laughing sound again. "It would please me if she, rather than any of the others, inherited."

"Anything else you can tell me?"

She took a slow deep breath. "A few weeks ago, saying she'd heard I was ailing, a woman who claimed she was a nurse at Seagate when the two Quintillion embryos were created, contacted me."

"Her name is?"

"Roberta Danford."

"Did you follow up on it?"

"Oh, yes. I made an appointment to call on her at her cottage in the Beachside Sector of the city. I'm still able to get around somewhat."

"And?"

"She was dead when I arrived, had passed away hours before. There was nothing of importance among her effects."

"What'd the autopsy show?"

"She died of natural causes."

"Nope, that's not right." He got up, started pacing around the dark brown rug. "A coincidence like that is unlikely."

"I agree, which is one reason I contacted your detective agency."

He walked over to the blanked windows. "Don't you ever look outside?"

"Not any longer."

He turned to face her. "Okay, Miss Quintillion," he said. "Gather together whatever background material you have on the whole mess. After I go over it, I'll work out some ways to approach Seagate. Seems to me I've heard it still exists."

"It does, yes."

"And I'll dig into the death of Roberta Danford. Those are places to start."

"Ideally I'd put you up here at the mansion," said the gaunt woman. "Since you have to keep being Batsford for a few more days, though, I fear you'll have to live in his home over in the Shelter Hills Sector. If you're lucky, you may not run into Betty Lou at all during your short stay."

"If I'm lucky."

CHAPTER 7

His secretary made an anxious yipping sound as Jolson came shuffling into his outer office. "It's four-fifteen, sir," exclaimed the plump green woman, rising up behind her licorice-tinted plaz desk and fluttering her right hand.

"Ah, thank you, Erna the Human Clock," he said in a nasty Batsford Quintillion tone.

She had a polka-dot scarf pulled tight over her bright purple hair. "Your cousin, Mr. Destry Quintillion, was of the understanding that he had an appointment with you for four on the nose, sir. He's been anxiously inquiring as to—"

"Fifteen minutes, old girl, makes not the slightest—"

"Will you get the hell into my office, you butthole, so we can talk?"

A broad-shouldered man of thirty in a three-piece gray bizsuit was filling the doorway, his tanned face rich with frown lines.

"Coming right up, Cousin D." Jolson moved toward him. "That hair of yours looks even more wretched up close, by the way, Erna."

"Yes, sir."

Not waiting, Destry went striding off along the glazwalled corridor.

Outside, the snow was still falling heavily down between the towers of the city.

"I've been kicking around what you said earlier, old cock," Jolson told the other man's broad back. "Seems to me that our agreement with Studs Gunny clearly guarantees us any and—"

"Thinking is *not* what I want from you." Destry hurried through his outer office, ignoring the lovely blue-skinned young woman who served as his private secretary and was waving a yellow faxmemo at him. He went into his private office.

Jolson took the memo from the anxious girl. "Urgent, is it, Effie?"

"Doubly so."

Destry was seated behind a stainless steel desk, scowling. "Don't go trying to romance my help."

Jolson carefully placed the yellow sheet on the desk top, smoothed it out. "A happily married man doesn't fool around with—"

"Peanuts," said Destry.

"Beg pardon?" Jolson sank into a tin chair facing the desk. The walls of the big room were blanked.

"How come you didn't know Studs Gunny was allergic to peanuts?"

"It's not in the specifications for our Shobots based on him."

"Doesn't your missus tell you the little quirks and peculiarities of the assorted bozos she—"

"See here, Destry!" Angry, Jolson stood and shook a pudgy fist at him. "I'm growing damned tired of your constant hints and allusions to Betty Lou's alleged—"

"A hint is subtle, Bats. I've always come right out and stated that Betty Lou is a tramp," he explained, grinning faintly. "The point is, Gunny is bitching because we licensed one of our Gunny Shobots to do a series of Bascom's Better Peanut Butter commercials out on a cablenet in the Hellquad planets. He claims his myriad fans know that he's allergic to peanuts in any form. They give him hives, the screaming meemies and—"

"You never do enough research, Des, and don't pay attention to what your underlings dig up." Jolson smirked. "Bascom's Better Peanut Butter doesn't contain a single peanut. That's why it's better. It's a complete synthetic, made of kelp and chemicals."

"Truly?"

He nodded. "Instead of howling at me, you might've—"

"Okay, okay. I'll get to his agents with this."

Jolson sat again. "Be a nice notion to tell the Bascom people about the allergy thing. They can tie it in with their spots. 'I can't not eat a bloomin' peanurt wiffout I get bloody blotches on me skin. 'At's why I ruddy well dote on Bascom's . . .' And so on."

"All right. Don't slump there looking so damned smug, butthole."

Jolson rubbed his ample chin. "During my recent jaunt to Barnum I got to thinking about Nanny Botz and wondering if—"

"Every time you thrust your noggin in a brainstim machine, you get soppy about that rattletrap piece of—"

"Be that as it may, I got to wondering where the old dear is these days."

Destry eyed him, hunching his wide shoulders slightly. "You really and truly have futzed up your wits, Bats," he said. "Nanny Botz has been stored in Warehouse 19 on the other side of town for years. As you well ought to know."

Jolson straightened up. "I guess I do know at that," he said.

A soft, silent snow fell through the twilight. Jolson, wheezing slightly, trudged across the private parking lot next to the multistoried brix building designated Warehouse 19.

The plaz ramp leading to the entry arch was smeared with snow. Before he'd climbed all the way up, the wide neoglass door whapped open.

"Reach for it," requested a piping voice from the dim-lit corridor beyond. "One false move, kiddo, and I'll fry your whizbanger and . . . Ah, oopsy, sorry there. Evening to you, Mr. Quintillion."

Jolson went lumbering across the threshold. "Still not wearing your lenses, Major?"

"They mar my looks."

"Your looks have long since fled, shrimp."

"Good thing I'm such a loyal employee, Mr. Quintillion, or I'd blow the whistle on you," said the dapper green midget, who stood with a kilgun still aimed at Jolson's crotch. "The Fair Play for Small People Guild frowns on such gibes, as do the Old Folks Antidefamation League, the Aging Midget Coalition, the—"

"Face it, Major, old midgets don't make comebacks. If you'd face the fact—"

"That's a show business truism, perhaps," admitted the emerald-hued Major Smalltime. "Yet I was once a star, playing all the great spots around the universe—the Hotel Maximus, the Orbiting Palace, Cosmo's, the Top o' the—"

"Spare me the golden memories," cut in Jolson, "and lead me to that sweet old companion of my happy youth, none other than Nanny Botz."

Verdant eyelids fluttering, the major swallowed and backed into the plaz wall. He tucked his gun under his glocoat, twisted at a vibrabutton. "Has nobody told you?"

"Told me what?"

Major Smalltime sighed, flapped his elbows twice, studied his yellow shoes. "Holy Toledo, I just now remembered. You been off planet." He turned his back on Jolson, went scurrying off along a twisting ramp. "Well, come on along. I guess I better show you the remains."

Tagging along after the midget, Jolson said, "Remains? That doesn't sound any too—"

"Best you prepare yourself for a shock. I know you were close to the old bim, but even mechanisms come to the end of their days." The major darted into a vast storeroom filled with standing androids and robots. "Most especially do they come to the end of their days if they get bopped on the dome with a spanner."

"Spare me any more of the sad details just now," requested Jolson, making a mournful sound and halting next to a long row of silent red-haired female androids. "To think that my faithful, kindhearted Nanny Botz is apparently no longer extant and—"

Bongo bongity bongity bongo!

He'd nudged the nearest mechanical redhead and her impressive bare breasts had lit up and started chiming. Tassels attached to the nipples commenced rotating rapidly in a counterclockwise direction and producing a harsh swishing sound.

Bong bong bongo bongity bong!

"This is hardly the time for such a lewd display." Jolson reached into the left armpit of the activated android, flicked the emergency cutoff switch.

"We got twenty-seven TV evangelists stored up on Floor 3A. I can coax a heartfelt eulogy out of any and all of—"

"Just take me to Nanny Botz."

The major, hands locked behind his back and head tilted, circled the stilled android. "She was one of the greats," he remarked. "Torrid Tessie Timberlake, known throughout the Barnum System as the Lass with the Musical Tits. Had chimes implanted in her yonkers so she could—"

"Where exactly have you got my old nanny?"

"In Workshop 5 on 3B." Taking a final look at Torrid Tessie, the major scampered off up another ramp. "You should've caught her act on Christmas Eve. Holy Toledo, but it was something. That quiff could play one dozen different seasonal carols on her knockers and each would bring a tear to the eye of young and old alike. Once I witnessed the Gay Bishop of Callisto himself blubbering into his miter like a—"

"Onward."

"Travel, I note, doesn't mellow you."

On the second level of the warehouse four dozen androids in blackface sat in neowicker chairs and strummed on banjos. "This happens a lot on wintry eves," explained the major as he guided Jolson across the storeroom toward another upward ramp. "These are sims of Mickens's Minstrels. Very big in the Hellquad System about eight, nine years ago. I keep scooting up here to deactivate them, but they turn themselves back on again. Sometimes there's nothing but 'Tell us, Rastus' and 'Is dat so, Mistuh Bones' until all hours of the—"

"File a report with Storage Management," suggested Jolson. "Might be it's time to mothball the whole lot of them."

"Aw, I'd hate to see that," said the major, starting up another ramp. "Sometimes they're company for me. A night watchman's lot is a lonely one. After a while you get to feeling these gadgets are your pals. A goofy notion, yet—"

"Golly gee whiskers, Major. I guess I really and truly am your friend, ain't I?"

"Yeah, sure you are, Fluffymuffin. I didn't mean to include you in my—"

"That makes me feel glad all over." A shaggy white robot hound had emerged from behind a row of standup comics and was trotting along beside the midget and Jolson. "You ought to ask those mean old Quintillions to give you a vacation, Major. Then you could mingle with real foks for a spell, and gee—"

"Scram," advised Jolson.

"Ixnay, ixnay," the major told the dog. "This is a Quintillion. Don't go antagonizing him, Fluff."

The dog's long red tongue came lolling out of his

mouth. "Heckodarn, Major Smalltime, I can't antagonize nobody," he said, giggling. " 'Cause I wasn't built that way. Nossir rooney. I'm the most lovable and lovingest little mutt what ever came skipping down the pike and into the hearts of kids of all ages."

"True," said the major. "You just sit here by this bunch of outmoded shock-rock singers. I'll stop and chat with you on my way back."

"Boyoboy, that sure sounds like fun. Don't it, Mr. Q?"

"Almost more than one dog deserves," said Jolson, moving on.

The major caught up with him. "Too bad that dog never caught on," he said. "He's been a real pal to me, but the public never took to him. As you probably know, we got nine hundred and sixty more of them down in Basement 6."

"I've been thinking that salty dogs are a pain, but—"

"How's that?" He cupped a green hand to his ear.

"Merely a philosophical remark that slipped out."

"Yep, I'm blurting those out all the time." The major darted through a wide doorway. "It's the solitude that does it. Least in my particular case. There she is, over in the corner there."

Jolson walked between two rows of workbenches, one of which held a spread-out android magician with his chest wide open. Slumped down in a glaz tube rocker was the body of a plump, matronly copper-coated robot. There were deep dents across her bosom and the left side of her skull was smashed in. Tangles of bright twisted wire and jagged pieces of shattered glaz stuck out through gaps in the surface. Her gray neowool wig was tilted and sat far down on her forehead.

"Who did this?" Jolson crouched, grunting in his fat man's voice. He rested a plump hand on one arm of the rocker. The chair started to tick slowly back and forth.

"Search me," answered the emerald major. "And I got to admit it's a blotch on my otherwise unblotched record. I returned from grabbing a cup of sinjo at a café around the corner five nights ago, see. The front door, which I always leave locked up tight, is flapping open, and I get a sense that things are going on wrong. You know, I almost didn't go out that night because there was one hell of a blizzard and I tend to get wafted away whenever there's a mean wind blowing. But I did and . . ." He paused, shrugged. "Somebody snuck in while I was out, and I wasn't away more than fifteen minutes. They bashed the old girl up in her parlor. She looked just like you see her now. Well, no, I take that back. Her rug was on the floor. I slapped that back on her coco. Even machines ought to have a little dignity when they pass on, you know."

Jolson stood. "You reported all this?"

"Sure, to Q-Mex Security. They sent a team over—one humanoid and two andies—and they nosed around. This was two days after it happened, by the way. They didn't find anything out."

"No other damage?"

"Not so you'd notice. And nary a thing swiped either."

Jolson shook his head, muttering, "Whatever she knew is lost and gone."

"If you want to know something the old bim knew,"

said Major Smalltime, "why don't you check with that brainchip copy of her brain?"

Jolson frowned at the major. "What brainchip is that, old sock?"

"The one," replied the midget, "you made for yourself last month."

CHAPTER 8

The hefty lizardman gestured at the client chair with the silvery kilgun in his right hand and mouthed, "Be right with you, chum." Hunching, he returned his attention to the pixphone atop his desk. "I really can't understand your attitude, Ethel. You've always been extremely fond of snerg casserole, and this one I prepared with—"

"I loathe snerg in any shape or form," came a voice out of the phone. "Once, when you still loved me, you kept note of my food preferences. Now, alas, I fear your attention is once again given over to capers and intrigues, leaving you—"

"Sweetness, how can you accuse me of—"

"Hang up," suggested Jolson from the other side of the desk. He'd remained standing, pudgy hands resting on the edge of the rubberoid desk.

"A little domestic discourse, be concluded in a minute, chum," whispered the thickset green man. "Here, take yourself a gander at my new brochure and park your toke." Setting his gun aside, he snatched up a faxpaper leaflet and tossed it at Jolson.

Race Doilycart, Private Eye was emblazoned across

the cover. *"A four-star op if there ever was one"—Sheriff Rune Beeweber, Estruma Territory. "He never sleeps"—Mrs. X, Satisfied Divorcée. Affiliated with the Universally Respected Briggs Interplanetary Detective Service.*

Instead of picking up the booklet, Jolson edged around the desk and poked the shutoff button on the phone. Then he clutched Race Doilycart's scaly wrist before the private eye could reach for his kilgun. "Attend to me," he advised. "AWJ426/HF5532/104P?"

"Glory be, you'll have Ethel thinking I hung up on her," lamented the lizard. "She's already in a huff about the dinner I left in the robochef for her to—"

"AWJ426/HF5532/104P."

"Your babbling isn't going to . . . Glory be, excuse it." Race Doilycart smacked his broad green forehead with the heel of his left hand. "That's a BIDS special ID phrase, isn't it? Yeah, if I wasn't so distracted by marital strife I'd have recog—"

"I have to use your sat/pix scramble phone to contact Molly Briggs on Barnum."

"AWJ426 . . . let me think, now. You must be Field Operative Ben—"

Brrrtttzzz! Brrrtttzzzz!

The big green private investigator flipped on the phone. "It was a complete and total accident, Ethel. A client happened to fall over onto the—"

"To think," came the crisp voice of the detective's wife, "that after but twenty-three months of marriage you would slam the phone down on me. Ah, and just two short years ago you characterized our relationship as one of blissful—"

"Hold on, love. I have to pick a client up from the floor." He rose up out of his rubberoid swivel chair.

"I can see that the snerg casserole was but the first sign of the total collapse of our . . ."

On tiptoe Race Doilycart escorted Jolson across his office and into a small side room. "Let me ask you a quick question," he said as he directed Jolson into a tin chair in front of a large sat/pix phone on a tin stand. "When you first ambled in, did I strike you as rough, tough and hard-boiled?"

"Nope." Jolson sat.

"Gesturing with the roscoe didn't impress?"

"Impressed me that you might well be a half-wit."

"Too obvious, huh? I pondered that," admitted the lizard detective. "It's difficult convincing prospective customers that you're hard as nails without risking looking the fool."

"Arguing about cookery with the missus doesn't help much, either."

"Exactly what I keep trying to convince Ethel, but she . . . glory be, I left her dangling on the pixie." He spun on his heel, dashed back into his office and slammed the door behind him.

Jolson punched out Molly's private number. A few seconds later the blank screen came to life. "So there you are, you frazzle-brained idiot. What's the big idea of flying the—"

"Snif, I've little if any time for pleasant chitchat with you. Put Molly on."

Sniffer squinted. "Is that you, Benny?"

"Go roll over and play dead. After you summon Molly to the phone."

"She's busy making a sandwich. Call back in a week."

"She'll have to interrupt her snack."

"The dear child is wasting away and yet you . . . Yoiks!" The robot dog dropped from sight.

"He's really been in an awful mood tonight." Molly was wearing a two-piece neocotton PJsuit, her long auburn hair pulled back and tied with a twist of green ribbon. "I've tossed him in the closet twice since you left, but then he starts reciting poetry about prison bars or singing ballads about union solidarity and—"

"I want you to do something for me, Molly."

"Yes, sure, certainly." She smiled. "Forgive my babbling. I mean, well, you've only been gone a few days, but I miss you already. So when I see you, even though you're still in that pudgy Batsford Quintillion persona, I . . . But, gosh, there I go again. Yes, what?"

"First off I'll give you a quick sum-up of what this Quintillion case is about." He then filled her in.

"Gosh, a missing heiress . . . or a missing embryo, anyway. That's sort of intriguing and exciting, especially with billions of trudollars involved. Looks like maybe I ought to hop out there to Murdstone to lend you a hand."

"Possibly later on, but right now I—"

"Couldn't you feign a mite more enthusiasm, Ben? What I mean is, I miss you and I assume that you, even though that may be a dippy notion, miss me as well."

"Right now I want you to talk to Batsford, use a truthdisc if you have to," Jolson told her. "His aunt Janella, our client, doesn't seem to know anything about this. But Batsford seems to have been digging into this before he embarked for Barnum."

"Digging into what—the mystery of the lost heiress, you mean?"

"I'll know more once I've gone through his stuff and locate a brainchip he apparently had made," said Jolson. "If he's already found out something about the Quintillion heiress, I want to know. Also why he's doing this and who he thinks may be opposing him."

"There's opposition, Ben?"

"Somebody murdered a robot," he replied. "Anyway, Molly, get right over to the Renfrew Brothers Detox Country Club and question the guy."

"Um." Molly glanced offscreen.

"Meaning?"

"Who would've anticipated he'd do something like that. I mean he was supposedly still stupefied, and the Renfrews have a top-notch secsytem. Even so, he—"

"He's not there? Batsford's on the loose, at large again?"

When she nodded, the motion caused the ribbon to shake free and her hair brushed at her shoulders. "Our fault for not putting a man to watch the place, but I figured—"

"When did he escape?"

"It's not exactly an escape, since he seems simply to have wandered off."

"Whatever you call it, when?"

"Two days ago."

"You've tried to trace him?"

"Of course. I'm not a complete ninny."

"And?"

She looked away again. "We tried all the brainstim

places in the Underbelly sectors, but he's not there, Ben," she said. "I went and talked to your friend Shadowland Slim and had to listen to Merle and His Magic Violin play a whole entire darn set. But we can't find Batsford Quintillion."

"If and when you find him, inquire about what he's been up to."

"Is this going to foul up your work?"

"No way of telling."

She nodded slowly. "What's Betty Lou Quintillion like?"

"I'm about to find out." Grinning, he ended the call.

CHAPTER 9

The hilltop mansion consisted of three opaque glaz pyramids linked together by great plaz tubes. The night snow hit the dark slanted walls and melted at once. Jolson was set down by his robot skycab at the edge of the one-acre estate.

"'Arve a narse ev'nin', guv," called the cab's voxbox as it rose up through the straight-falling snow.

Tugging off his right mitten, Jolson trudged to the high gate in the brix wall surrounding the grounds. He was approaching the whorl-scanner when he noticed the gate was standing three feet open.

He glanced around, saw nothing but snow on the grounds. Pulling the neowool mitten back on, he pushed through the opening and onto the wide thermopath.

As he came nearer Batsford Quintillion's mansion, Jolson spotted a thin rectangle of light in the otherwise blind facade of the central trylon. He slowed, removed both mittens, stowed them in a flap pocket of his all-season greatcoat. Reaching into his shoulder holster, he brought out his stungun.

The light spilling out into the snowy darkness was a

pale orange in color. The neoturf welcome mat had a Q cut into it. Jolson halted on the tail of the letter, narrowed his eyes and hunched slightly, looking through the open doorway.

About twenty feet along the hallway a body lay sprawled flat on its back, booted toes pointed ceilingward.

After taking a deep breath, Jolson stepped inside. "Not a choice location for a snooze, Jorrocks, old bean," Jolson said in his best Batsford voice.

The android servant, who'd met him at the spaceport on arrival, didn't respond.

Carefully Jolson approached the spread-eagled form. "Damn, more servo-bashing." Someone had used a disabler on Jorrocks—a powerful one, judging from the sooty singe marks across the white front of his shirt. Then something heavy and metallic had been used on the mechanical servant's skull. It was badly battered and one plaz eye lay on the peach-colored thermorug.

"I must say, this isn't the sort of reception I was anticipating." He walked a few steps beyond the body and called out, "Betty Lou? Are you here?"

Nothing came back at him but silence.

He nodded, going over in his head the layout of Batsford's home. He'd memorized the mansion's floor plans during a briefing in the BIDS offices back home on Barnum.

Down this corridor and left into another one.

He did that.

Then use the fourth door on the left. That'd be Batsford's den, and the most likely place for him to conceal a dupe of Nanny Botz's brainchip.

The dark neowood door stood half open.

Jolson booted it all the way open, dived into the den in a low crouch. He straightened up, muttered, "Holy Toledo."

He was confronted by himself.

Sitting behind an ivory desk was another Batsford Quintillion. This one had a neat kilgun wound just to the right of his heart.

Jolson was about to move toward the dead man when a great deal of mechanical hooting and wailing commenced in the night sky just above the mansion.

"And now cops," he observed.

By the time Jolson got back to the main hall a lean catman and an android were there, both kneeling beside the remains of Jorrocks.

"You're not dead, huh?" inquired the catman, rising up.

"You needn't sound so unhappy over the fact, Detective . . . ah . . . your name eludes me."

"Considering the times you've poked your conk into a brainstim box, I'm surprised you can still recall your own handle," said the catman. "As usual, I'm Detective Ripperger of the Capital City Police Squad."

"I fear," said Jolson, making a guess as to why the officer had visited him before, "that Betty Lou and I have been having another little tiff. Neighbors pixed you again, did they?"

"Matter of fact, Quintillion, it was your cousin Destry. Says he's been trying to phone and your pixies are on the bum. He got concerned and buzzed us."

"We're a very close family."

The android was a handsome, aquiline-visaged humanoid in a conservative three-piece neotweed bizsuit. "Ah, a clue," he exclaimed, holding up a blonde hair. "A definite clue, Rip."

"Cease calling me that."

Jolson said, "Have I met your machine on previous occasions?"

Snarling, the cat detective answered, "No, nope. He's new, brand new. The commissioner went and bought sixteen of these bozos at an Anticrime and Detection Equipment Trade Show last month. Stuck me with this one."

"A crime of passion, don't y'know," said the android as he got to his feet, "or my name isn't Inspector Volto, another fine product of the respected ForenTech Corporation of Murdstone."

"Shut your bazoo for a spell, Inspector," advised his reluctant partner. "Where's your missus, Quintillion?"

"She went off into the night," replied Jolson with a sad shrug.

"Hot pants can foul up most anything," observed Ripperger.

Jolson said, "Well, I certainly appreciate your dropping in, old cork, but as the hostilities have ceased, why—"

"We'd better make casts of these footprints," decided the android, pointing at the rug.

Kawang! Kawang! Kawantz!

"What's that odd noise coming out of your associate, Detective Ripperger?"

"The inspector can mix his own plaster, inside his innards somewhere."

"Ah, how fascinating."

Kawang! Jiggyjiggy! Kawango!

"As for you, Quintillion, I'd like to hear you explain how a spat between you and your lady led to this valet of yours getting himself iced."

Jolson lowered his eyes. "It's a sad story."

"Tell it anyway."

"Sometimes, when Betty Lou is in one of her moods, she tends to get a bit suicidal."

"A bit is right. Like the night she threatened to dive off the apex of the manse here, wearing naught but an all-season teddy. Or the fun-filled occasion when she claimed to have swallowed six full bottles of snerg tranquilizer and—"

"This time she implied, purely in jest I'm sure, that she was going to blow her brains out," explained Jolson. "Poor brave Jorrocks took her seriously and tried to wrestle the weapon away from Betty Lou and—well, you can see with what result. Thank you once again for dropping by. It's heartening to know our police force stands ever—"

"Your pixphones?"

"Eh?"

"How come they don't function?"

"Ah, yes, that." Jolson nodded. "I fear I am the one who must take full . . . Say there, Inspector, don't do that."

From a nozzle in his left thumb the android was spurting bluish plaster out on the rug. "Can't be helped, sir," answered Inspector Volto. "This is, after all, a murder investigation and—"

"Quit that and tidy up the mess," instructed Ripperger. "It's not a murder if an andy gets bumped off.

Now, Quintillion, explain about the pixies going flooey."

"In aiming a well-deserved kick at my mate," Jolson said, "I missed her backside entirely and busted a pixscreen. Causing the whole system to go out, I guess. You know how things can—"

"No, I've never kicked a phone."

"You're more even-tempered than I." He took hold of the catman's elbow. "Thank you for stopping in and . . . Forget about cleaning up your plaster, Inspector Volto."

"Deuced odd, what? I intended to suck the stuff up, but succeeded only in spitting out more. Beastly mess, but if you'll allow me to send over a—"

"Go wait in the skycar," his partner told him.

"Yes, by jove, I do believe that's the wisest course." Avoiding the plaster, he toddled off outside.

Jolson guided the catman toward the doorway. "Do pass on my good wishes to the commissioner and all the—"

"About the maid?"

"How's that, old sock?"

"There's a defunct andy maid, arse over teakettle, in your shrubs out front."

Jolson raised an eyebrow. "Those hedges happen to be my pride and joy. I do hope there's been no serious damage to—"

"Who used a kilgun on her?"

"Ah, there I can only guess, Detective Ripperger. I'd venture to say it must've been Betty Lou on her way out."

"Another suicide attempt?"

"Most likely, or perhaps she was just in a temper."

"Good night, Quintillion." Ripperger left, kicking the door shut with the heel of a boot.

Jolson waited five seconds, then hurried back to the den.

CHAPTER 10

It took Jolson seventeen minutes to go over Batsford Quintillion's den, and six more to locate the pixphone central switch and turn all the phones in the mansion back on. Then just under five minutes more to route a call from here through Race Doilycart's sat/pix scramble setup to Molly Briggs back on the planet Barnum.

Sniffer answered again. "I'm in no mood for guessing games. Simply inform me which of the many Batsford Quintillions you happen to—"

"Fetch Molly, Snif. This is Jolson."

"Do you have any notion what these interplanet calls are costing, beanpole? Can't you scribble your slipshod field reports on a faxgram and post them via—"

"Molly. Now."

"Honestly, Sniffer, I'm going to have to bolt you in a closet again unless . . . What is it, Ben?" Molly replaced the robot dog on the screen.

"Letting a surly hound answer your damn phone all the time doesn't reflect well on you," he said. "But that's not why I called. The—"

"Don't you think I'm forever telling him not to do that? But every darn time the thing buzzes, Snif goes galloping for it like a herd of wild grouts and—"

"Ah, such pitiful small thanks I get for wearing my paws to the nub in the service of truth, justice and—"

"Shush. Ben, you look uneasy. Or is this just part of your Batsford persona? Speaking of him, we—"

"I found him."

"Where? There?"

"Yep. For some reason he came home to Murdstone, back here to his mansion."

"Well, for *what* reason? Can't you get him to explain what in the heck he's—"

"Somebody killed him. A few hours ago."

"Golly." She slumped in her chair, ran a hand through her hair. "It could've been you, Ben. What I mean is, there you are going around as an exact replica, thanks to the exceptional abilities and knacks you picked up while serving as a Chameleon Corps agent, of Batsford Quintillion. It's just probably chance that you aren't defunct and Batsford isn't making this report to me. Or . . . gosh, do you think they *know* you're impersonating him and knocked him off under the impression they were getting a BIDS operative?"

"Not sure," he answered. "But I'd guess whoever did it was after the real Batsford. After they shot him, they went through his papers, popped his safe. Some of his papers seem to be missing, and there's no trace of the copy of his old robot nanny's brain that he had made."

"This all doesn't sound very good. It's not going to help your investigation into the whereabouts of the missing Quintillion heiress."

"Yep, these latest events have set me back a bit," he admitted. "Were you able to find out anything about him—what he did on Barnum, why he flitted from the detox spa?"

"Batsford left Barnum very soon after he slipped away from the Renfrews," Molly said. "They maintain he was still moderately stupefied. Could be he got a crackpot notion he had to return to Murdstone right quick to help his aunt Janella."

Jolson said, "Get in touch with her and explain what's happened. Obviously I'm going to cease to be Batsford. I'll contact her later when I set up a new identity and a base of—"

"Whoa there. I have to know who you're going to be next so I can keep in touch."

Jolson reflected for a few seconds. "I'll be Hungry Jack Graustark, residing at the Ice Palace Hotel here in the capital of the territory."

Her nose wrinkled. "Isn't the real Hungry Jack a despicable, loathsome toadman who practices the con-man trade in the seedier territories of—"

"That's the very Hungry Jack I'll be, yes. I happen to know he's spending a hiatus in an out-of-the-way detention station orbiting one of the Trinidad planets."

"Couldn't you, once in a while, impersonate somebody wholesome?"

"Wholesome people aren't much of a chall—"

"Batsy? Batsy, honey baby love? Batsy, where the thundering doofap are you, lover?"

Jolson said, "Sounds like my wife's come home. Call our client and I'll—"

"Ben."

"Yep?"

"Don't do anything . . . tacky. Please?"

"That has been one of my mottoes throughout life. Never, if at all possible, do anything tacky. Bye." He killed the phone, sprinted to the shut door of the den, opened it and eased into the corridor.

"Batsy? Hide-and-seek isn't a favorite sport of mine, honey bunch. Where the blinking dofiddle are you?" someone was bellowing in the vicinity of the living room.

"Coming, love. Coming right away," he called out, and started to trot.

"As though we weren't in hock enough already," the lovely young blonde in the scarlet sinsilk teasesuit was saying while she paced the immense living room. "We owe the Shrub Doctor ninety-six thousand trubux, we owe Love Doctor Emerzon a hundred and four thousand, to name a few. You owe Cosmo's four hundred thousand in gambling debts."

"I know, I saw the IOUs in the den."

"What? What are you muttering about, Batsy?"

"Nothing, love."

"Give the poor sap a break," suggested the plump blond man lounging in the glaz slingchair. "Lay off him, for pete's sake."

"Button your lip, Cousin Rudy," said Betty Lou. "Now, back to you, Batsy. We aren't enough in the hole without your going and ruining poor dear old Jorrocks—well, actually, I never could stand the flipping old swish. The point is, jeez and a half, he costs two hundred and sixty thousand trubux and we still owe sixteen dofapping payments on him."

"Love, I can have the Q-Mex techs patch him up. Along with Marie."

"What the flapdoodle is wrong with my maid?"

"It must've been vandals, love. They up and shot her with a kilgun, then tossed her in the shrubs out yonder."

"Do you realize we still owe over a hundred and seventy thousand trubux on her? Do you further realize we owe the Shrub Doctor and Snippers, Inc., a combined total of seventy-three thousand trubux for the care and upkeep of those flipping hedges?"

"Give the poor simp a break," advised the languid Rudy Quintillion, crossing his plump legs and gazing at the glaz ceiling. "On top of which, kiddo, you're forgetting why we dropped in."

"Like thunder I'm forgetting." Hands on hips, she glared at Jolson, who was perched on the edge of a tin armchair. "I tried to pix you, Batsy, but all the farping phones are down. What did you do, boot one of them again in a fit of—"

"Vandals again, my love."

"Vandals seem to have had a fricking busy night."

"Sure, that's what vandals do," said Jolson, smiling blandly at her. "They go around vandalizing."

"Cousin Rudy and I and your poor cousin Camilla, who's waiting for us at the shuttleport, were all set to hop up to Cosmo's when I remembered that you have no more credit there." She held out a beringed hand toward him. "So I need some cash. If you hadn't futzed up the fripping pixies I wouldn't have had to come all the way out to this dump, which you know I hate, just to get—"

"Betty Lou, my own, I'm really afraid I haven't any cash to spare for—"

"You had a whole stewpot of cash in your safe last time I peeked. If you won't hand any over, then I'll get some myself." She started for the doorway.

Hopping free of his chair, Jolson planted himself in her path. "That money's all gone."

"How can it be gone?"

"Vandals."

"They vandalize, they don't steal."

"That's what I tried to tell this bunch, but to no—"

"I'm going to take a look anyway, because—"

"If you do, love, I'll poke you in the snoot."

She snorted. "Yes, you would, wouldn't you? I'm glad Cousin Rudy is here to witness how you—"

"Matter of fact, ducks, I think I'll wait outside in the landcab." Cousin Rudy left his seat, heading for the way out. "Nice seeing you again, Batsford. Pity I don't get into Q-Mex much, or we could have lunch. But then I rarely arise before four in the afternoon and that's an awkward time for lunch, or so many people seem to feel. Be seeing you."

When he was gone, Betty Lou said, "I really intend to get some cash, Batsy. So you'd better—"

"I have to ask you some questions," said Jolson, "and get some truthful answers. This won't hurt."

"What's that dingus you just slipped out of your pocket?"

"Called a truthdisc." He slapped it against her throat, held on until it took hold.

CHAPTER 11

The vidwall turned itself on at exactly 7:00 A.M. "Once again it's time for the planet's most popular and informal news hour, *Wake Up, Murdstone.*"

Jolson groaned, sat up in his wide floating airbed and gazed across the bedroom of his hotel suite. He was Hungry Jack Graustark now, an obese and pale green toadman.

"C'mon, Jeanmarie, grab your sox. We're on the air." On the vast video screen a handsome humanoid with wavy golden hair was leaning over a rumpled jellobed, nudging someone hidden by a tangle of blue neosilk sheets.

"Take a leap, Sam."

"No fooling, Jeanmarie. It's time for *Wake Up, Murdstone.*"

"It's time for *up your kazoo!*"

Chuckling, Sam yanked the sheets free.

A naked young black woman was revealed atop the bed. She muttered but did not stir.

The handsome man, who was wearing just the top portion of a polka-dot PJsuit, said, "We've got a lot of big stories to cover, including a brutal murder in the capital of this very territory. Fact is, Ramon Hudsud is standing by at the scene, the modernistic mansion of Q-Mex heir Batsford Quintillion, and waiting to give us an exclusive on-the-scene report."

"So let him report while I snooze."

Jolson thunked out of bed, lumbered over to the bureau and picked up his bug detector. Eying the screen now and then, he checked his suite for any spy devices.

"This is Ramon Hudsud reporting from the lawn of the Batsford Quintillion manse," a small lizardman was saying. "You'll notice, Sam and Jeanmarie, that the box hedge immediately behind me has suffered considerable damage."

"Right, Ramon. Looks almost as though somebody fell over into it."

"Can you two pansies gab a little more quietly? I got a terrific hangover this morning and—"

"You had lots of fun at the grand opening of the new lounge up at Cosmo's orbiting night spot last night, huh, Jeanmarie?"

"Stuff it, Ramon."

There were no bugs. Jolson settled into a floating plazchair to concentrate on the news report.

". . . Quintillion's body was discovered early this morning by his lovely gadabout wife, Betty Lou Quintillion. Her team of physicians won't allow her to talk to our *Wake Up, Murdstone* cameras, but we are given to understand that the charming grieving widow told the police her husband was murdered by vandals. Detective Ripperger of the Capital City Police Squad confirms that Batsford Quintillion had been called on last evening by the police. When we asked Detective

Ripperger about the excessive amounts of plaster found in the mansion, he declined to—"

"Enough." Jolson turned off the wall and rose.

Waddling into the bath unit, he studied himself in the full-length mirror. He shrugged and stepped into the airshower compartment.

"Betty Lou didn't have anything to do with the murder," he said to himself. "And she doesn't know anything about who might have killed her husband. But she did know something about why Batsford came home early and why he had a dupe of Nanny Botz's brain. So I got something out of using the truthdisc on her."

He left the stall, wandered into the bedroom and dressed in a handsome three-piece lemon-yellow glosuit. Crossing the room he stepped into the dining alcove and patted the tabletop printshop unit sitting there.

Someone rapped on the suite door.

Jolson was wheezing when he reached the spyhole in the door. Out in the hotel corridor stood a copper-plated robot in a heavy plaid overcoat. "Ah, yes," Jolson said, opening the door, "you are no doubt the house dick."

"Ice Palace Hotel security officer," corrected the robot, inching into the suite. "Cash Cardigan's the name, Mr. Graustark."

"And what is the purpose of this early visit, my boy?"

"I've found out who you are."

"Oh, really?" From the breast pocket of his glowing jacket he extracted a fat kelp stogie and lit it. He then returned his hand to the vicinity of his shoulder holster.

"You happen to be none other than Hungry Jack Graustark."

"The desk computer knows that already, my boy." Jolson let go of the butt of his stungun and took hold of his cigar.

"Hungry Jack Graustark," repeated Cardigan. "But what the hotel doesn't know is that you're one of the rottenest, slimiest, no-good, low-down scoundrels on the face of the planet. It's a disgrace to a fine hotel such as this to have such a disreputable con man within its walls."

"Is this an eviction, my good man?"

"Not exactly, no. It's rather a request that you bribe me to allow you to remain."

"Ah, then that's no problem at all. Remain right here on the threshold." Exhaling smoke, he strolled to the alcove and gathered up a handful of freshly printed stock certificates. "Each of these certificates, my boy, of which I am bestowing ten upon you, appears to be at this time only worth a paltry ten trudollars each. Very soon—sooner than you might expect, were I at liberty to divulge all the inside information I possess—soon, I assure you, each will be worth at least ten times the face value. And, if you hold on to them, as I heartily advise you to, they shall provide for you handsomely in your old age."

"Well, I appreciate that, Hungry Jack, but the thing is, I'm a robot. So technically I won't ever have an old age. What I'm more interested in is cash money right—"

"Rather that's what you *were* interested in until this

fortunate encounter between us, dear Cardigan. Now, having attended closely to me, you no doubt realize that these shares in Consolidated Skymines are worth much, much more than mere cash. Indeed, they're also worth more than gold, silver, precious stones and even snerg pelts."

"You really think so?"

"There is not the slightest doubt in my mind." He thrust the decorative certificates into the house detective's metallic hand. "No need to thank me now, my boy. In later years, though, when you're dwelling in the lap of luxury as a result of this chance encounter—why, pause, pause and think not too unkindly of poor old Hungry Jack Graustark. Now scram, I've got a guest."

A green man about five foot four in height had come striding along the maroon all-season hall carpet. He wore a two-piece strawberry-hued funsuit with neon lapels. "Take your time in bidding adieu to this animated gaboon," he said. "I get portal-to-portal pay."

Cardigan squinted down at the newcomer. "You look familiar."

"He's the senior geologist for Consolidated Skymines," explained Jolson, shoving the robot out of the room and tugging the green man in. "No doubt you've seen his photo in the prospectus."

"No, that can't be it. Because until a few minutes ago I'd never heard of Consol—"

"You'll want to check the morning stock report coming up on *Wake Up, Murdstone,*" he said, giving the house detective another helpful nudge. "It's due on any moment. You'll just have time to get back to your office and catch it." He shut the door.

"Don't you ever get tired of these masquerades, Jolson?" inquired the green man as he settled into a floating armchair. "Thirty years as a Chameleon Corps agent, now as a private peeper for—"

"Twenty years with CC," Jolson corrected. "And it's the pleasure of working with folks like you, Facts-on-File, that makes my work so satisfying. What have you got for me?"

From a side pocket of his jacket, Facts-on-File drew a folded sheet of maroon faxpaper. "My bill. Six thousand trubux, payable in advance."

"C'mon, you can send BIDS an invoice, Facts."

He smiled a small smile. "As the leading provider of siphoned data on this planet, Jolson, I can't openly do business with a legitimate concern like BIDS." He fanned himself with the bill. "Six thousand, in cash."

"Okay, here." He lifted his vast rump, fished out a groutskin wallet and took six blue-and-gold thousand-trudollar bills from it.

Lunging, Facts snatched the money and replaced it with his bill. "Odd coincidence," he said, settling back in the chair. "Just last evening you pix me about some members of the Quintillion clan, and then this morning I hear tell a scion of the family got shuffled off by vandals."

"The entire universe thrives on coincidence, my boy." He took a final puff of his stogie before tossing it into the nearest floor dispozhole. "What did you get for me from the various data sources you have access to?"

"Okay, as to Dr. Amos LaChance. He's defunct—correction, he's on ice," said the information siphoner. "I had to tap into two government sources and a *Re-*

tired Physicians Recreational Newsletter subscription list to get all this. Seems Dr. LaChance was suffering from Ellison's syndrome, for which there is as yet no known cure. So he had himself put into a suspended-life state and stored away until such time as a cure comes along. For the past six and a half years LaChance has been stored away in a joint commonly known as the Cooler—over in Zelado Territory. Interesting that the old gent used to be associated with the Quintillion family many years ago."

And interesting, according to what Betty Lou had told him, that Batsford Quintillion had been trying to locate this onetime director of the Seagate Clinic. "Another of those strange coincidences that give spice to our lives. What about Lucky Quintillion?" That was the other individual Batsford had been anxious to track down.

"A contemporary of Dr. LaChance. If alive, he'd be in his seventies."

"*If* alive?"

"Alonzo 'Lucky' Quintillion was the black sheep of the family, a title there's been keen competition for over the years," explained Facts. "A ne'er-do-well, he went through a great deal of money before the family heaved him from its bosom. He spent his later years inhabiting many of our better skid rows. Vanished, supposedly, about five years back."

"This isn't sounding like six thousand trubux worth of information."

"Hold on, Jolson," said Facts-on-File. "Even his family lost track of him, but I was able to run down an account of a possible sighting only a year and a half ago. In an unpublished yarn a free-lancer tried out on the *Galactic Inquirer.* That's the sort of stuff I'm nifty at digging loose."

"A year and a half ago isn't my idea of recent."

"Lucky Quintillion was seen over in the Torrid Zone, a fiery desert area some thousand or so miles to the south of us," the siphoner said. "Were I you, I'd check on a colony dubbed Bumland. It's a sort of last-chance setup for derelicts on the edge of the Torrid Zone."

"Derelicts don't always last a year and a half."

"Listen, I'm still in the process of gathering more material on these guys. By tomorrow or so I ought to have more." He left the chair, slipping the cash into an inside pocket. "I'll pass whatever I get on to you for only a minimum extra charge. What more can you ask?"

"Hardly anything," said Jolson.

CHAPTER 12

Early in the morning of the final day of the week Jolson boarded a flying bus bound for Zelado Territory. He was still in his Hungry Jack Graustark mode.

The Skytours bus sat alone at the far end of the skyterminal field, a rattletrap crimson craft with snow heaped high on its sagging roof.

There was no one inside save the driver, a lean owlman in a too-large gray unisuit. "Shit," he remarked as Jolson came grunting aboard.

"How's that again, my boy?"

"Now we have to make this dim-witted flight."

Several of the frayed neoleather seats had suitcases, boxes, baskets and packages piled atop them. "Are there no other passengers?"

"Naw, and most mornings we get to cancel this early-bird skybus flight. All that crap on the seats is just a little cargo I haul on the side," explained the morose driver. "No rush on any of it."

Jolson settled his bulk into a seat midway back. "Had I not urgent business in Zelado, my good man, I'd disembark and allow you to return home to bed."

"Sure, that'd be great. Me trying to sleep in the same goddamn bed with that dim-witted wife of mine." Sighing, he pulled the door-shutting lever. "Some dames snore, others babble in their sleep, and a few groan and moan. But Loretta sings light-opera ditties. Ever try to sleep with that going on?"

"Once in a theater orbiting Pluto."

"Not the same." The owlman lifted a black lunch box from his lap to the floor next to the driveseat. "Ever have cold pizza for breakfast?"

"Not often."

"Loretta's trying this new cold pizza diet . . . Did I mention she weighs in at two hundred and eighty-seven pounds? Alls we got around the house at the moment is cold pizza." He started up the engine of the skybus. "That's what I got in the lunch box. Cold mushroom and grout sausage pizza. That and six bananas. Loretta used to be on that banana diet and we got a lot left over."

The Skytours bus began to shimmy; all the cargo quivered. Mournful whines filled the aisle. The engine grumbled, rumbled and then feebly roared. The craft, shedding snow, taxied across the rutted field. It rattled wildly, lurched, rose into the overcast morning.

"Welcome aboard Skytours Bus No. 232," said the owlman, placing a wrinkled cap on his feathery head. "I'm your driver/pilot Groucho Krigbaum, and it'll be my pleasure to ferry you to your destination and answer any and all inquiries you may have as to scenic wonders and points of historical interest." He coughed into his fist. "Actually, I have to say that bullshit, it's in our contract. If it's all the same with you, I'd just as well you keep your goddamn questions to yourself.

Anyhow, there aren't enough scenic wonders between here and Zelado Territory to stuff in a snerg's ear. As for history—about a hundred years back, somebody massacred a bunch of wogs at the base of Deadman's Peak. That's about it."

"You certainly live up to your nickname, Groucho my boy." Jolson took out a kelp cigar.

"Shit, that's no nickname. My dim-witted parents actually christened me Groucho," explained Krigbaum. "That can affect you, you know, having a stupid first name. It seemed a portent and a prophecy in my case."

"Ever think of changing it?"

"Yeah, and I used to talk it over with my two brothers, Nervo and Henpecko, but they convinced me I'd be breaking with family tradition and my heritage. So I stuck with Groucho."

Lighting the foul stogie, Jolson puffed and slouched in his seat. A large neowicker suitcase sat on the seat directly opposite him, and he had the fleeting impression the suitcase was watching him.

Shaking his head, he blew out smoke and contemplated the morning landscape they were flying over. Below, there was nothing but sooty fields of snow.

After several minutes of flight Krigbaum said, "Should you want a slab of cold pizza or an overripe banana, just let out a holler."

"I enjoyed a lavish breakfast before I took my leave of my hotel, but thanks all the same."

"You going to Zelado for the skiing?"

"I thought I might indulge a bit. In spite of my size, I am an avid sportsman."

"No shit? I wouldn't of guessed it. You look to

weigh more than Loretta, and that dame's about as active as a truckload of . . . Ah, well, shit. I'm really pisspoor with similes and metaphors." The driver shook his head, shedding a feather. "The point being, she is no sportswoman."

Jolson puffed on his kelp stogie.

Krigbaum said after a moment, "Do you recall me mentioning Deadman's Peak?"

"I do indeed, Groucho my boy."

Krigbaum jumped deftly free of his seat, grabbing up his lunch box and yanking it open. "Well, this crate is now set on a robot course smack for that mountain," he announced. "It'll hit in exactly four minutes, Jolson my boy. That ought to discourage any further snooping on your part."

Jolson's scaly green hand had started for his shoulder holster.

But Krigbaum already had his stungun free of his lunch box.

Zzzzummmmmm! Zzzuuu . . . frizzlefriz . . . zzitt!

"Crap, they stuck me with a screwed-up weapon."

The stungun beam that hit Jolson's broad chest was sufficient to cause pain to go needling through his body. He swayed, sat back down, slumped and fell out of his seat into the aisle.

"Let's hope the goddamn skybelt they provided me can be depended on." Opening the skybus door, Groucho Krigbaum leaped out into the chill gray morning.

Jolson was not completely stunned. He struggled to move, to get control of himself. He didn't succeed.

CHAPTER 13

The neowicker suitcase became agitated. "Jeez, I am really and truly growing weary of saving the necks of ninnies and yobs," complained a voice from within.

"Sniffer," murmured the sprawled Jolson.

The lid of the suitcase popping open with a creak, the robot dog emerged and jumped out. He landed, on all four hard metal paws, smack in the middle of Jolson's back.

"Oof," the partially stunned ex-Chameleon managed to say.

"Ah, these races against time surely add zest to life," observed Sniffer as he went trotting along the aisle toward the controls of the hurtling skybus.

With considerable effort Jolson pushed himself up to a sitting position.

Deadman's Peak, a formidable frozen monolith, seemed to be rushing very swiftly at them.

"Unk," complained the chrome-plated hound. "Some dolt left a wedge of cold pizza on this seat. That ain't classy, nay."

Using his right forepaw, Sniffer took over control of

the suicidal Skytours bus. The aircraft shuddered, bounced and then went shooting up on a perpendicular course.

Jolson slid down the aisle, collecting dust and discarded food wrappings. When he thunked against the rear seat, a heavy hatbox jumped off and bonked him on the skull.

The skybus leveled off, clear of the mountain. Sniffer said, "Once again superior wits and stamina have saved the day."

"Much obliged," said Jolson, and passed out.

Molly was sitting beside his bunk, watching him anxiously. "I'm really glad you're not dead."

"A sentiment I can share," he replied, finding his speech a bit slurred still.

"Um . . . let me ask you a somewhat intimate question," the auburn-haired young woman said carefully. "How's your backside?"

Jolson considered. "Feels as though somebody thrust several sharp needles into it."

"Tra-la," commented Sniffer, who was curled up on a throw rug before the blazing fireplace. "Very gratifying to have one's handiwork receive recogn—"

"Snif insisted on administering some shots," explained Molly, reaching out to touch Jolson's scaly green forehead and then deciding against it.

"Standard procedure for reviving a stungun victim," reminded the dog. "Holy crow, since I've got all this nifty medical gear built into me, it's dumb not to—"

"Go out and sit on the sun deck," ordered the young woman.

"Snow deck, you mean. Land sakes, child, there's a near blizzard raging out."

"Well, at least withdraw to the living room of our chalet."

"All the great medical geniuses have met initially with scorn and ingratitude."

"You have my undying gratitude," Jolson told the departing hound.

"With that and a trubuck I can buy a faxpaper."

Molly leaned closer. "You don't, do you, have to keep on being this repulsive Hungry Jack?"

"Nope, especially since the opposition knows I've been posing as him."

"What opposition?"

Concentrating for a moment, Jolson changed back to his true self. "Okay, that's better."

"Um . . ."

"What?"

"You're still green."

He held up a hand. "So I am." Gradually he caused the emerald tint to fade away. "Aftereffect of getting stungunned. Futzes up my control a mite."

Molly asked, "What opposition are you alluding to?"

"Possibly you can tell me," he said. "The feathery lad who tried to turn the skybus into a suicide express called me Jolson. Nobody knew that except you and Sniffer. Well, you and Snif and Facts-on-File. But he—"

"As I recall from my briefing before embarking for Murdstone, Facts-on-File is a sleazy lowlife who makes his living mostly from selling stolen information. Seems very likely he'd betray you for a—"

"Nope, I trust Facts."

"You trust him, yet accuse me of—"

"Who'd you tell about my being at the Ice Palace as Hungry Jack?"

"No one. Well, what I mean is, no one except our client, Janella Quintillion."

"Leak could've been on her end, I suppose."

"It's much more likely, really, Ben, that your paid informant is—"

"Next explain why you're here."

"Honest to gosh." She pushed back her chair, causing it to make a harsh scraping noise across the realwood flooring. "I mean, here we jump onto an express flight from Barnum, with barely enough time to pack sufficient crimebusting gear and a sufficient wardrobe, and come out to this second-rate planet to—"

"Third rate."

"Hush. I get Sniffer planted on the very skybus you're booked on and I trail along in a rented skyracer—one that costs me nine hundred and fifty-six trudollars each and every day I keep it. We save you from a fate worse than death . . . Well, no, actually we save you from death. And afterwards you act annoyed that I'm here at all. Not that I expect a word of thanks for all I—"

"Thanks," he said. "But why'd you come out here when you did?"

"For one thing, I felt you were in need of some backup help, and darned if I wasn't right," she said. "I also got a sat/pix call warning me that things might be much more dangerous for BIDS here on this planet that we dreamed."

"Who phoned?"

"She claimed to be Dr. Natalie M. Jenga, head of R&D at Q-Mex. A plump birdlady in her middle fifties."

"Claimed to be?"

"I suppose it was she who contacted me. Since we arrived last night, though, we haven't been able to locate her."

"What's our client say about Dr. Jenga?"

"The doctor suggested that I tell nobody about her calling. So I haven't discussed it with Janella Quintillion or anyone else at Q-Mex."

Jolson propped himself up on his pillow and glanced around. "Where are we?"

"This is the Skull Mountain ski area." Molly gestured at the small viewindow. "Hence all those snowcapped peaks outside. I rented us a chalet—to the tune of fourteen hundred a day."

"I was en route to a place called the Cooler, which ought to be about thirty miles north of here," he said. "Dr. Amos LaChance, onetime head of the Seagate Clinic, is there."

"Then you can talk to him about—"

"Not sure. He's in a suspended state, awaiting a new medical breakthrough."

"Was he somebody Batsford was interested in?"

"Yep. It's likely that Nanny Botz put Batsford on to him."

Molly was thoughtful for a moment. "The people working against us—whoever they are—will try to stop you from contacting Dr. LaChance."

"That may well be what the bus business was about," he said. "On the other hand, they may've simply wanted me dead and thus unable to hunt for any missing Quintillion heiresses."

Molly eased her chair closer to the bunk again. "I've really been very concerned about you," she admitted. "When Sniffer landed that runaway skybus and I saw you looking as though you were dead . . . Well, it unsettled me. Gosh, I don't know. Maybe it's just space lag, but I always feel much more attracted to you when we're not on our home planet."

Reaching up, he put a hand on her shoulder. "Nothing more that a job-related side effect."

"You think so?"

"Beyond a doubt." Pulling her close to him, he kissed her.

CHAPTER 14

Sniffer was at the controls of the sleek white skyvan. Making a pleased cackling sound, he sent the aircraft swooping low over the complex of domed buildings that made up the Murdstone Cryptobiosis Center, better known as the Cooler. After executing a whooshing bank, the robot dog landed the van on a stretch of pink pastel parking area. "Now that's aerobatics of the highest—"

"This is absolutely the last and final time you ever," Molly told him as she tucked a stray strand of hair back under the nurse's cap, "ever fly any craft that I am—"

"That's the beauty of traveling with an expert stunt pilot," explained the dog. "You *think* you're in dire peril, yet all the while you are actually as safe as a—"

"Remain here," instructed Jolson. "Alert. You may be called upon to do some expert evasive flying to get us clear of the Cooler."

"A snap."

Jolson was clad in a two-piece white medisuit. He was younger and smaller now, twenty-eight years old and barely five foot four. Cherubic-cheeked, he possessed sandy hair and a winning smile. "You're not to leave the ambulance and the ambulance is not to leave this field," instructed Jolson, stepping out into the chill, windy afternoon and turning to help Molly from their skyvan.

"Two things I want to say before we enter this place," she said, halting at the lip of a ramp leading to the central dome of the Cooler.

"Heck, you can say anything you want, Nurse Jayne. Just because Dr. Floyd Christmas is the most famous physician in the entire Barnum System, why, that doesn't mean he hasn't time for a friendly chat with his employees. Nossir." Slipping an arm around her waist, he gave Molly an enthusiastic hug.

"That's part of it. Just because I got all maudlin back at the chalet yesterday and allowed you to kiss me a few times, and, well—there's no use denying it—I sort of got in your bunk with you there for a few minutes. I still believe that while we're on a case we ought to maintain a—"

"I'm Dr. Floyd Christmas, Nurse Jayne. And, hey, don't you read my best-selling books? They're on all the lists on all the planets in the universe just about. What do I advocate in my books? That hugging is good for you." He hugged her again.

"Okay, that brings me to the next point. What worries me is that Dr. Floyd Christmas *is* a celebrity. He could pop up on the vidwall while we're trying to pass you off as—"

"You don't keep up with *Galactic Publishers Weekly.*" He guided her up the ramp. "Five months ago Q-Mex built sixteen android replicas of Dr. Christmas to cope with all his publicity and public appearance chores. Nobody hereabouts is likely to know where the real one is."

The plaz door whispered open. The lobby was cream-colored and circular. Seated behind a semicircular plaz desk was an apeman in a two-piece medi-suit. He glanced up from the seed catalog he'd been perusing, squinted at them, then started to laugh. "I say, what a bally impressive stunt, Dr. Christmas, old chap."

Keeping his arm around Molly, Jolson approached the shaggy receptionist. "Hey, I see you know me. But then, who doesn't? Dr. Floyd Christmas, author of *How to Live Forever—Or Even Longer.* The certified top best-seller on ninety-six planets, fifty-six asteroids, forty-three space colonies and—"

"You know I know you, old thing," chuckled the apeman. "You gave me a big hug not more than ten minutes ago. And, you know, it did make me feel good all over, so I suppose there's something to be said for your philos—"

"Oops," observed Molly.

"You think you saw me a few minutes ago?"

The receptionist nodded. "You didn't have this deucedly handsome young lady with you then, though. A decided improvement, I might say."

Sighing, Jolson said, "This is just as I feared. It must be he, wouldn't you think, Nurse Jayne?"

Molly said, "Um . . . Well, yes. Yes, it would have to be, wouldn't it."

Leaning an elbow on the desk, Jolson said, "This alleged Dr. Christmas asked to see a certain Dr. Amos LaChance, didn't he?"

"He told me that Dr. LaChance was his favorite

professor at medical school and—Jove, are you implying that—"

"It was my crazed twin brother who posed as me earlier. Edmond 'the Slasher' Christmas."

"I never heard that you had a brother, old man."

"One's not likely to brag about a brother, twin or otherwise, nicknamed the Slasher."

"I say, I think we jolly well better summon the sec staff and have them throw the net over this chap before he—"

"No, no. We came prepared to handle him, and it's better I take the risks." He nudged Molly. "You brought his medication?"

"Oh, yes, I always carry a supply, for just such occasions as this." She patted her white shoulder bag.

"How do we reach Dr. LaChance?"

"To get to his storage bin, you go down that second corridor over there, up the ramp to Level 3. You'll find the old boy, along with a few others, in Cubicle 36A," said the receptionist, leaning and pointing.

"You've nothing to fear," Jolson assured him as he and Molly went hurrying off.

Molly was into the small shadowy room first. "That's enough fooling around."

A Dr. Floyd Christmas was in the process of sliding a seethru glaz coffin out of a row of them in midwall and hefting it onto a floating lab table.

Molly yanked up her white skirt, reached for the small stungun in her thigh holster. "Just start backing away from—"

"Duck," warned Jolson, diving for the floor.

Dr. Christmas had snatched a gun from the table and was aiming it at the young woman.

Zzzzzzuuuuuummmmmmm!

Jolson fired his stungun.

The beam smacked Dr. Christmas in the chest, causing him to gasp, bark and go jigging into a wall of bins. His hand swung down to his side and a ray of sizzling purple light shot from his gun.

Zzzzzitttzzzzz!

A hole about the size of a saucer was eaten in the plaztiles.

Dr. Christmas's knees clanked together, his legs went limp, and he knelt, swayed, fell over on his face and hit the deck with a thumping clang.

"Not the true Floyd," decided Molly, putting her gun away and smoothing down her skirt.

"One of the Q-Mex sims."

"It's sure starting to look as though Q-Mex is tangled up in this whole mess, doesn't it?"

"There's a strong possibility that such is the case." He eased the door shut, crossed to the fallen android.

"Praise Saint Reptilicus! Praise Saint Serpentine!"

"Golly, it's Dr. LaChance." Molly nodded at the coffin. "The andy must've reactivated him."

A chubby old gentleman, his head thickly covered with crinkly white hair, was sitting up in the glaz box and making pleased sounds. From a pocket in the jacket of his candy-striped PJsuit he extracted a breath-fresher spray and squirted it in his mouth. "That feels better," he said in a still-creaky voice. "I assume some scientific genius has finally found a cure for Ellison's syndrome and so you two admirable medicos have brought me back to life after a slumber of . . . um . . . exactly how long have I been—"

"The present situation is somewhat more complex than you imagine," Jolson informed him.

"How's that, young man? Well, no matter, help me out of this danged box and then we can—"

"When you hear what we have to say," interrupted Jolson, "you'll probably want to stay in the box, Doctor."

Molly shifted in the pilot seat of the skyvan, looking back over her shoulder to frown at Sniffer. "I don't mind your sulking," she told him, "but do it a heck of a lot more quietly."

"Groan," replied the robot hound, who was lying on a passenger seat on his back in a dead-dog pose, paws pointing stiffly up at the low white neometal ceiling.

"We should've put him in storage at the Cooler," said Jolson, who was sitting next to Molly. "They could've done it when they put Dr. LaChance back into his trance."

"Poor man, such a disappointing day for—"

"Here you have a gifted mechanism who knows more about aviation than a whole flock of migrating grackles," complained Sniffer, "and you reduce him to cargo status."

"Maintain silence," advised Jolson.

Molly sighed. "We didn't learn one heck of a lot from Dr. LaChance, even after you stuck that truthdisc on him," she said. "Though I suppose that's to be expected, since Ellison's syndrome causes loss of memory and—"

"We found out that LaChance was bribed by Lucky Quintillion way back when," reminded Jolson, who had returned to his own identity for the moment. "That was to allow our black sheep to make off with the second Quintillion embryo. Apparently Lucky was planning to demand ransom from his family for the safe return of the other heiress."

"Planned, but somehow never did." Molly shook her head, glancing out at the bleak afternoon they were flying through. "It's also possible that old Doc LaChance just isn't remembering clearly enough what actually—"

"My guess is that the late Nanny Botz also either knew he and Lucky were in cahoots or strongly suspected it," Jolson said. "Which is why Batsford was interested in these two gents, LaChance and Lucky."

"Next we have to locate Lucky."

"I do, yep."

"Wait now, Ben, we're a team. What I mean is, I jaunted out here to Murdstone to help out, and I think we ought to stick—"

"Members of a team don't all play the same position," Jolson told her.

"Jeez," muttered Sniffer, "sports-derived analogies already."

"Hush. What are you getting at, Ben? Are you suggesting that I—"

"If Lucky Quintillion is still above the ground, he's in Bumland. Hell of a lot easier for me to infiltrate that spot than—"

"Heck, there are plenty of lady bums. I'm not a shapechanger like you, but I can pass myself off as—"

"Nope, what you have to do is find Dr. Jenga," he said.

"We can find her after you and I—"

"We're being anticipated and competed with too damn much on this case."

"I don't think there's any way they could've known you were going to pass yourself off as Dr. Christmas to get into the place where poor old LaChance is stored," said Molly, shaking her head. "It must've been a coincidence that they sent a Dr. Christmas andy into the—"

"Probably. My point is, this Jenga woman maybe knows something we ought to know. About the missing heiress or about why we're being outfoxed and—"

"Let this skinny gink wallow with the deadbeats, Moll," said Sniffer. "You and I will locate the elusive Dr. J., find the lost heiress, save the day and end up giving Jolson the fingeroo."

Molly said slowly, "Oh, probably that is the best plan—not about the obscene gesture, but locating this darn Jenga woman."

"I do enjoy these board meetings so," said Jolson, slouching further in his seat.

"Nertz," remarked Sniffer.

CHAPTER 15

Jolson was not himself. He was instead a long, lanky man of fifty some years, wearing a faded pair of blue jeans, a tattered plaid shirt and a jagged-brimmed farmer's straw hat. Slung over his narrow knobby back was a dented twelve-string guitar.

He came shuffling up to the neowood gate in the low fence around Bumland just at sundown, with a hot dry desert wind rubbing at him and trying to jerk the hat clean off his gray head.

A one-armed robot wearing the jacket of an old city cop uniform was sprawled in a neowicker rocker on the other side of the weathered gate. His left eye was gone from the socket, his right blinked faintly red in a jumpy, irregular way. "Top o' the morning, pilgrim," croaked the robot.

The twilight wind sent a swirl of gritty sand spinning around the two of them. "Wellsir, to my way of thinkin', she's nigher to sunset," drawled Jolson. "But, shux, I never much argue over temporal matters."

"You and me both, pilgrim. What can I do you for?"

"I'd like to mosey on into Bumland."

"Voluntarily?" With his one hand he gestured behind him at the scatter of transplanted hovels, tenements and run-down stores that stretched away on his side of the fence. "You'll no doubt get rounded up and dropped here sooner or later. Might as well not rush the . . . Hey, wait there, pilgrim. I know you."

"Mighty lots of folks do, yep."

"Sure, sure." The guardbot started to clap his hands, then realized he was short one. "Long time back, before my own fall from grace, I was a secguard at a whole stewpot of theaters. You used to appear at some of them. You're—"

"Tunky Nesper," announced Jolson.

"That's you, yes. The Sweet Singer of the Spaceways, the Wayfarin' Balladeer of the—"

"I'm that there Tunky Nesper, for certain."

"There was a song of yours I used to especially like." He scratched at his ball of a head. "Something about a welfare check."

"That's a little ditty I made up name of 'Ever' Time I Move to Jupiter They Still Keep On Sendin' My Welfare Check to Mars Talkin' Blues,' " supplied Jolson, scratching his crotch left-handed and kicking his snub-toed shoe at the hot sand. "Now, partner, I'd be right obliged if you was to open up them there portals to let me on in."

"Sure thing, even though I can't figure why you'd want to visit a hole like—"

"Wellsir, now, I'll tell you. To my way of thinkin' the Good Lord up an' give me a talent for singin' an' pickin'," said Jolson, watching the ramshackle robot rattle free of his rocker and unlock the gate. "When you got a talent, why, shux, you got to share her, especial' with fellers down on their luck."

"We sure got a stewpot full in that category here in Bumland, that's for sure."

Jolson shuffled through the opening. "Much obliged, friend."

"Think nothing of it, Tunky."

Touching the brim of his hat in a lazy salute, Jolson started into the derelict enclave. The hot wind kept after him, nipping at his dirty bare ankles, tugging at his shirttail, keeping him dry and gritty.

Looming up on his right was a five-story brix tenement. A fragment of street sign that was still attached to the facade indicated that this particular structure had been transplanted from a slum sector on the other side of the planet. A drunken catman wearing only a pair of raggedy warm-up pants was sleeping on a stretch of cracked sidewalk, his matted left paw clutching an empty nearwine pouch. He cried out in his sleep, shuddering, grip tightening on the pale green plaz.

In the doorway of the building a dead ratman was propped in a sitting position, the flesh already half gone from his face and arms.

An immense shadow suddenly formed on the dusty twilight street. Taking a dodging step to his right, Jolson stared up.

Flying low over Bumland was a rusty green skyvan. Stenciled on its rutted underbelly was DERELICT EXPRESS—KEEPING OUR CITIES SCUM FREE!

"Goodness me, will you please, really, keep out of our flight path."

A glistening glazbottomed tourist skyvan was gliding over the dusky enclave, heading directly for the slower van.

"Out of the way," said the pilot over his comsystem. "Honestly, you people ought to know . . . Ah, just a moment, ladies and gentlemen. I've spotted a celebrity stumbling along the mean street directly below us."

The tourist-laden skybus dropped down, hovered directly over Jolson. An amber spotlight blossomed and caught him in a bright circle of light.

"I was right, folks. You're looking down on a man known throughout the universe for his rambling ways. None other than Tunky Nesper, the fabled Footloose Minstrel of the Galaxies."

"Nothing like making an unobtrusive entrance," muttered Jolson, grinning bleakly up at the skybus and tipping his battered straw hat at the ogling tourists. "Right pleased to meet you all." Hunching his lean shoulders, he continued on along the darkening street.

The *Derelict Express* was settling into a landing in the square as Jolson rounded a corner. It hit the ground a shade too hard, sending up gritty clouds of dust, nearly colliding with the dry fountain at the square's center. A wide dented door in the side of the van shrieked open and a dozen ragtag, baggypants derelicts came tumbling out into the new darkness: a thin birdman in a once-white funsuit, four stupefied catmen, an assortment of toadmen, lizardmen and humans.

"Damn it, you've up and done it again. I keep telling you you've got to screen these people better than—"

"Futz off, lady." The door of the van whapped shut; it rattled and chuffed, then rose up into the night.

The tall young woman stood watching, hands on hips. Her hair was nearly the same shade as Molly's. She was pretty, in an athletic, outdoorsy sort of way, and wore the dark blue uniform of the Salvation Commandos.

Jolson ambled over. "What's eatin' on you, miss?" he inquired.

"It simply doesn't help things when they dump dead ones on us." She pointed at a sprawled birdman with the toe of her boot.

The other new arrivals were mumbling, grunting, complaining and tottering to their feet.

"He's gone on to glory for sure," agreed Jolson, squatting by the feathery dead man.

"And it's very evident that he was already dead when they gathered him up to transport here." She knelt close to Jolson, slid a tanned hand under the dead man's raggedy shirt. "Now the Salvation Commandos will have to stand for a funeral, spending funds we really can't spare. Let's see what it says on his godtag." She tugged out a small worn nickel disk and squinted at it. " 'I am a practicing member of the Church of the Latter-Day Sea Cooks.' Ah, that's very unfortunate, since they insist on burial at sea. Well, it'll have to be worked out." She rose, wiped her palms on her trousers. "I'm Sergeant Suicide Sally. And you?"

Shaking the proffered hand, Jolson answered, "Most folks call me Tunky Nesper."

Suicide Sally laughed, inhaled. "That's marvelous. We have several of your vidalbums at the Mission Fortress. People who've dropped to the lower depths seem to enjoy your tunes," she said. "What brings you to Bumland, Tunky?"

"Wellsir, miss, I'm sort of like that there tumbleweed back out there in the desert," he drawled, scratching at his ribs. "I just sort of blow along where the wind takes me. But, shux, I figure as how you get as much out of life that way as you do iffen you made yourself a real official itinerary."

Suicide Sally nodded. "You're absolutely right."

"Course, I was kinder hopin' that I'd also run into an old pal of mine," added Jolson, kicking at the dust. "You been stationed hereabouts long doin' your good works, Sally?"

"This is my second year."

"Then maybe you heard of an old friend of mine name of Lucky Quintillion."

She said, "Now isn't that strange?"

"Can't tell if it is or it ain't, since I ain't exactly sure what you're gettin' at."

"Excuse me for being less than explicit," apologized the Salvation Commandos sergeant. "I was simply alluding to the fact that a gentleman claiming to be a Welfare Squad agent was here only yesterday inquiring after your poor friend."

"Claimin' to be?"

"Well, he was young, handsome and dapper. Frankly, he didn't seem anywhere near frazzled and weary enough to be with the Welfare Squad."

"So you didn't cooperate?"

"There wasn't much I could do anyway. I simply informed him that Lucky Quintillion had passed away some six months ago, peacefully in his sleep. Lucky was well advanced in years, as you know."

"Dang, he's dead and gone, huh?"

"Yes, and I know it's often difficult to accept the death of someone who—"

"It's just, Sarge, that I done had my heart set on talkin' with the old feller at least once more."

"You're too late for that," said Suicide Sally. "But you might get some consolation by having a little talk with Rev Upchurch."

Removing his disreputable hat, Jolson knuckled his scalp. "Who might he be?"

"He's an ordained robot minister in the Church of Saint Reptilicus," she replied. "Your late friend was converted to that faith in his last months, went to confession with Rev almost every day."

"Did he, for a fact? Yep, that must've give him a lot of peace of mind, talking about all he'd done in the past that he felt guilty about, unburdening himself of all his darkest secrets and shames." Jolson spit in the gutter. "Did you send this dapper feller to Rev Upchurch?"

"Oh, no, certainly not. He wasn't in the need of any spiritual consolation, and I didn't trust the man at all."

"I'd be mighty obliged, miss, if you was to tell me how to get to this religious mechanism."

"We can go visit him together as soon as I take care of this unfortunate dead person. Will you help me carry him to our SC morgue?"

"Nothing would give me more pleasure, miss."

CHAPTER 16

The thickset gatorman tourist dropped a trudollar coin into the plazcup attached to the wheezing accordion of the blind birdwoman.

"Bless you, kind sir." The hot wind rustled the neostraw flowers on her hat.

"Afraid I need more than that." The tourist leaned closer. "I'd be obliged if you could provide me with a receipt, signed, dated and witnessed. Ever since my tax audit last year I . . ."

"Rev Upchurch holds his services in a storefront just around this next corner," explained Suicide Sally, leading Jolson past the blind woman and the tourist.

"I sure got to tell you how downright obliged I am to you," he said. "Seems like no matter what corner of this ol' universe I'm ramblin' through, why, folks is always real dang nice to me."

"It's gratifying to be able to do a favor for the Golden-Throated Folksinger of . . . just a second." Drawing a stungun, she fired into the alley they were passing.

Zzzzzzzzummmmmmmmm!

"Mugger," she explained.

Someone fell over back in the shadows.

Around the corner and half a block farther along, a glaz door flapped open and two tattered ratmen came sailing out. They got tangled and entwined in midair, landing in the gutter next to a dead dog.

"Still say he's got cheese in there," grumbled the first ratman, stumbling to his feet.

"Sure he has." The other rose, rewinding his soiled muffler. "You can smell it from out here even."

"And what might you want?" A white-enameled robot in a black cassock was blocking the doorway and scanning Jolson.

"Nothin' but a few kind words."

"But not cheese?"

"Rev Upchurch," said Suicide Sally as she took hold of Jolson's arm, "allow me to introduce Tunky Nesper."

"Ah, yes, the Bold Balladeer of the Starways. Come in, sir."

Jolson sniffed while crossing the threshold. "Does smell a mite like cheese hereabouts," he said, glancing around the small room and its rows of straightback chairs.

"This was a cheese shop before being transported here. The smells, alas, linger."

"Your congregation's on the small side this evening, Rev," observed the Salvation Commando.

Two catmen were dozing up near the front of the room. The rest of the seats were vacant.

"A slow night in the Lord's business, yes."

Jolson said, "Sal tells me as how you knew my pal Lucky Quintillion."

The ballhead nodded. "That I did, Tunky. He was a man burdened down with many past sins."

"Now, Rev, that's sort of what I wanted to jaw with you about."

The religious robot said, "Would it be worth a donation to the church to you, Tunky, to learn what you wish to learn?"

"Five hundred trubux."

"A thousand."

"Six hundred."

"Nine hundred."

"Seven hundred."

"Eight hundred."

"Seven hundred and fifty tops."

"That'll do some of the Lord's work anyway," decided the robot. "Come back into the sacristy and we'll talk."

Jolson patted Suicide Sally's backside in an avuncular way. "Much obliged for your help, missy," he said. "You can go on about your good works now."

Rev Upchurch shifted in his gunmetal chair, patted his enameled head and eyed Jolson's guitar. "Members of my order always speak what's on their mind," he said. "Which is why I am bound to mention that I can't abide your sort of folk music. Many of my parishioners, however, are fond of your—"

"Shux now, Rev, this here now gitfiddle ain't for playin'." Chuckling good-naturedly, Jolson opened a panel in the backside of the instrument resting on his knee. "I actually carry all sorts of interestin' gadgets inside here."

"That gimmick you're extracting looks suspiciously like a—"

Bonk!

Jolson had slapped the small parasite control box to the top of the robot's skull. " 'Scuse me for bein' in such an all-fired rush, your holiness," he said. "But I just ain't got time for polite jawin' and chattin'. You're now under my control an' you got to answer all my questions."

"I . . . Yes, I do seem to be obliged in that direction."

"Did Lucky Quintillion ever tell you about a missing embryo?"

"Yes."

"What was his involvement with it?"

"In his younger and less moral days, Quintillion had stolen the embryo from a place called the Seagate Clinic," answered the mind-controlled robot. "There was some connivance on the part of a highly placed employee of the institution; a bribe was exchanged. Quintillion made off with the embryo of one of the Quintillion heiresses, carrying it in a special life-support container."

"What was his plan?"

"The poor sinner told me that he then bore an enormous grudge against his family for slights against him both real and imagined," answered Rev Upchurch. "He intended either to sell the embryo to some of the family for a ransom of three million trudollars or to destroy it. That was something he was sure many of the other heirs would be glad to pay almost as much for."

"Far as I've been able to determine, Quintillion didn't do either of those things."

"That's because he was arrested shortly after stashing the container in a safe hiding place. This was on a charge having nothing to do with the theft of the embryo. He spent the next fifteen years on Devil's Island No. 19, a penal colony that orbits—"

"I know right well where they all are. What about the embryo?"

"That remained safely hidden away until he was released."

"Where is it now?"

"Ah, Tunky my son, that makes for a strange and pitiful tale."

"Get busy tellin' it."

"Something like twenty-five years ago, Lucky—who by the way failed most of his life to live up to that nickname—entered into a high-stakes poker game. When his funds were gone, he wagered the Quintillion embryo and—"

"You're tellin' me the half-wit lost the Quintillion heiress in a goldang card game?"

"Exactly, yes."

"Who won the thing off him?"

"A disreputable toadman named Leroy Cashdollar."

"Damn, now I got to go trailin' him down all to heck an' gone."

"That won't be necessary."

"You know where Cashdollar is?"

"I know what the man did with the embryo. And I am compelled to tell you."

"That you are. So get to it, Rev."

"Lucky and Cashdollar encountered each other right here in Bumland about a year ago. Cashdollar, too, had fallen to a new low," continued the robot. "At any rate, he confided in Lucky what he had done with the stolen embryo."

"An' that was?"

"He'd sold it to an outfit called Baby, Inc. They supply children for the childless, using surrogate mothers, orphans, whatever they can lay hands on, including embryos."

"Was the embryo planted in a surrogate?"

"Yes, something like twenty-three years ago."

"Do you know what happened to the child that was born?"

The parasite control box rattled slightly when Rev Upchurch shook his head. "That I do not, nor did Cashdollar."

"Where's Baby, Inc., located?"

"Some eleven hundred miles to the south of us. In Azedo Territory."

Jolson frowned. "They're all lunatics over there."

"Their racial attitudes are a bit backward, but since Azedo Territory controls a great deal of the tropical fruit consumed on Murdstone it's been felt wise not to—"

"I'll have to make my way over there."

"I hear they don't take kindly to drifting folksingers."

"Shux, I won't be one by the time I hit the border," said Jolson, grinning.

CHAPTER 17

Jolson took advantage of the rioting.

Matter of fact, he'd arranged for it and had hired the three dozen noisy protesters who were demonstrating down in the courtyard of the Borderland Hotel. From the one-way glaz window of his room he could see the assortment of militant birdmen, catmen, dogmen and toadmen who were chanting slogans, shaking fists and brandishing signs—FAIR PLAY FOR NONHUMANS!, MAJOR BOULDERWOOD MUST GO!, etc.

When Jolson learned that the major was stopping here, he knew he had a way to get across the border into Azedo Territory.

"That skinny toadman with the false whiskers isn't quite convincing enough," Jolson observed, turning away from the view. "But most of the others are okay."

He took a quick look around the room, nodded and grabbed the groutskin attaché case he'd purchased in the lobby luggage shop earlier this morning.

Jolson was now a handsome, sun-brown blond young man in a conservative two-piece purple bizsuit.

He eased out of the room, hurried along the corridor and tapped politely on the door of Suite 316.

Four seconds later a deep, rumbling voice from within boomed out, "I intend to fight to the death, you filthy Nons!"

"Er . . . I . . . er . . ." mumbled Jolson. "I . . . er . . . suggest you turn on your spyhole, Major."

"How's that, son? Ah, yes. Good notion, shows keen thinking."

Jolson fiddled with his yellow bow tie, smiling nervously at the eye in the door. "I'm . . . er . . . Marcus Glass, Major," he explained very politely.

"Marcus Glass?"

"From across the border, you know. Er . . . Governor Lilly sent me to . . . er . . . get you out of the situation that's arisen here."

"Ah, clever bit of strategy on his part, yes."

The door whirred, clinked, shivered, swung slowly open.

Major Bazooka Boulderwood was a large, red-faced man of sixty-two. Wide-shouldered, sporting an impressive bristling gray mustache and wearing a snug three-piece paramilitary bizsuit and a beaked cap of military cut.

Jolson gave him another shy, polite smile, held the attaché case up to his chest and whispered, "I've brought you . . . er . . . a little something in the way of funds, sir."

"Eh? How's that, son? You'll have to speak up. Hearing's a bit shot after years of combat. And with all those Nonnies howling down below it's—"

"This is some under-the-table loot for you," shouted

Jolson, stepping into the major's suite and kicking the door shut. "You apparently don't recall our last meeting. I'm with Governor Norvell Lilly's Illicit Fund Disbursement Office. I have here in this case a hundred thousand trudollars to aid you in your work and . . . er . . . to make your impending visit to our territory even more enjoyable."

Major Boulderwood reached for the attaché case. "I always enjoy my speaking engagements in Azedo," he said, starting to scowl over the fact that Jolson wasn't turning the case over to him. "Only rational and sensible territory on the whole damn planet, if you ask me. Humans first—that's a sensible policy. If only all of Murdstone shared those values I wouldn't have to wear out my toke making speeches and . . . Son, are you going to give me that money or not?"

"Er . . . not here, sir," said Jolson apologetically. "No, what I've been instructed to do first is get you safely out of this besieged hotel and across to Azedo Territory. I know you didn't plan to embark for my home territory until tomorrow, but what with these violent demonstrations, it's been decided to sneak you away from here right this—"

"A few blasts from a stunner," said the major, face increasing in redness, "will settle all their complaints." He gestured at an array of stunguns, stunrods, blasters and kilguns laid out on his floating sudomarble coffee table. "We might even kill one or two, that way teaching those Nonnies that—"

"Er . . . Governor Lilly would prefer you didn't kill anyone just yet, Major," Jolson told him. "The media over here tends to exaggerate these little incidents all—"

"Reporters can be shot, too," the major reminded him.

"They are annoying, but slaughtering them can create an image problem. Especially now with our Humans First Party rally and formal dance about to take place in Azedo Territory. Your speech will be the high point of the entire—"

"Still and all, son, Major Bazooka Boulderwood isn't the sort of fellow to run out on a fight. Especially when he's facing a rabble composed entirely of Nonnies." He frowned deeply. "Do you by any chance know how I came by my nickname of Bazooka? Well, son, it was in—"

"Every schoolchild knows that tale, sir. And every schoolchild, in Azedo Territory at least, reveres you and your legend." He smiled once more, opened the case and reached into it. "I think, however, that when you see what I have here, you'll agree it isn't the time or place to tangle with the crowd."

"Money, is it, son?"

"Not exactly, sir." Jolson yanked out a stungun.

Zzzzzummmmmmm!

Jolson went marching across the lobby of the Humans Only Ritz, elbowed a baggage-laden catman bellhop out of his way, pushed through the revolving glaz door out into the glaring afternoon street.

He was a ringer for Major Bazooka Boulderwood, who was stashed away in a cavern back across the border and not due to awaken for another forty-eight hours. Tugging at his mustache and squaring his shoulders, Jolson started briskly off along the wide pastel pavement. The broad thoroughfare was lined with high palm trees; the air was hot and muggy.

A plump toadwoman flower vendor fainted suddenly from the heat and fell in a soggy heap directly in his path. Jolson stepped over her, muttering, "Damn Nonnies. No stamina."

He strode by the imposing glaz exterior of the Azedo Territory headquarters of the Daughters of Certified Humans, turned a corner and had to dodge to avoid colliding with a thickset green man who was bending over to drink from a Toads Only public fountain.

Jolson's face grew even redder and he aimed a kick at the man's wide backside.

The kick missed by about three inches. Jolson muttered, regained his balance and continued on his way.

At the next corner three catmen were lined up waiting to use a Cats Only public toilet that stood in the intersection.

As he passed an arched alleyway, he heard a rustling. Reaching into his paramilitary jacket, he touched his shoulder holster and slowed.

"Major Boulderwood?"

"You are Major Bazooka Boulderwood, aren't you?"

Three hooded figures emerged from the shadows into the yellow haze of the afternoon street.

"I damn well am Major Boulderwood," asserted Jolson, scowling and keeping his hand on the handle of his stungun. "And any Nonnie lover who thinks he or she is going to—"

"Don't you know who we are, sir?" The young woman, wearing a two-piece black cazsuit and boots, lifted off her black sinsilk hood. "We're all members of the Ladies Auxiliary of the Hooded/Mounted Anti-Nonnie Storm Troopers."

"Ah, yes, to be sure." He brought his hand back into view. "Didn't recognize you without your mounts."

"Well, there's a sad story there," said the unhooded one, a slim blonde of about twenty-three. "Just because we missed a few payments, we lost our grouts."

Another of the hooded ladies removed her mask. She was redheaded, near forty. "Only three or four payments behind, we were, but they sent a repo squad right to the storm trooper stables to—"

"The path of the Human Supremacist is often strewn with obstacles." He started to inch away from the trio.

"Major," said the blonde with a tentative smile, "the last time you were here in Azedo you made us a promise."

"Did I indeed?"

"You promised to tell us," said the redhead, "how it was you came by your Bazooka nickname."

"Ah, my dears, and a stirring narrative it is. To hear it, however, you'll have to attend my upcoming speech," he said. "Now I must be off on an important mission."

"Wouldn't you like an escort?" inquired the blonde. "We look fairly impressive, even without our grouts."

"I appreciate the offer, but this particular task requires a bit of secrecy and stealth, something difficult to achieve if accompanied by three damsels with hoods over their heads." He saluted them smartly, turned on his heel and hurried off.

He cut across a sun-drenched little park, ducked the spray from a Frogs Only drinking fountain and turned into a narrow, quirking lane.

When he pushed through the low white gate in the low white fence around the pink and blue Baby, Inc., cottage offices, a pleasant nursery tune came tinkling out of speakers sunk in the bright green neoturf lawn. A single dove, one-eyed and sooty, was perched on the slanting red shingle roof.

The white neowood door tinkled, then swung open for him. A rival tune commenced once he'd crossed into a charming blue and pink parlor.

"Wellsir, welcome to Baby, Inc., Mom and Dad," said a motherly voice coming out of three speakers planted in the pale blue ceiling. "We just know you'll find the little one you seek right here in our cozy headquarters. To start things rolling, Mom and Dad, let's take care of the initial consultation fee. That's only a thousand trudollars. We accept all major banx cards. Just slip yours into the slot in the bunny rabbit's tail."

Jolson slid out a nontraceable banx card, thrust it into the rear end of the metallic rabbit perched on a pink pedestal in the middle of the parlor.

There was a whirring, a distant tinkling.

"Very good, parents-to-be. Step through the door that's opening on your left and follow the polka-dot arrows to Interview Room 3."

Jolson stepped through the pink wall. He went, however, not to an interview room but down into the underground file rooms of Baby, Inc.

The aircirc system in the rented landvan was producing low keening noises. When Jolson again whapped the control panel with the heel of his hand, the metallic wailing intensified for roughly twenty-five seconds and then subsided.

The jungle roadway he was traveling along was growing rapidly darker as the day ended. The roadlights came on automatically, illuminating the insects, who were coming out as night fell.

Nodding, Jolson set the vehicle on an automatic course for the Azedo Skyport, which lay two hundred miles to the southwest. He unbuckled his safety gear, slid over into the passenger seat and punched up a number on the special scramblephone mounted in the dash.

"Buckle up," admonished the van's voxbox.

Jolson complied.

"I shouldn't have to tell you these things."

The screen went from gray to black to multicolored. Molly appeared. "Yes, what?" She was looking back over her shoulder.

Jolson was using his own persona at the moment. "Just reporting in, boss."

Rowdy ragtime piano music could be heard in the background.

Molly said, "Oh, darn. Forgive me for sounding snippy, Ben. Sniffer, stop that racket right this minute."

"Are you noticing the left hand work, Moll?"

"Quit," she advised the unseen robot hound. "He's been pounding the piano in our suite for over an hour. And wearing a little plaz derby at a cocky angle."

"Why not pack him in a soundproof crate and ship him back to the manufacturer for a refund?"

The piano music died.

"I'm glad you called," said Molly. "I mean, I'm always glad to see you—and find out you're still alive."

"I feel good about that sort of news, too, knowing I'm alive. Now, the reason—"

"See, we're about to take off for Cosmo's. You know about that—"

"Yep, it's that enormous casino and resort that orbits this planet."

"That's it," said Molly. "Sort of mysterious in a way, since nobody really seems to know who Cosmo is. Is he a person, a conglomerate, an andy, a computer?"

"Why are you heading there?"

"Because I have a tip that Dr. Natalie M. Jenga is there. I'm still darn anxious to talk to that lady."

"She's at Cosmo's of her own free will?"

Molly shook her head. "My informant thinks she's being held prisoner in one of the posher resort sectors of that satellite colony."

"May be a bit rough for you if you try to—"

"Honestly, Ben. As I keep telling you, I'm a perfectly competent field operative and I—"

"Listen," he cut in. "You probably won't have to shuttle up there at all."

"Whyever not?"

"Because I've found out who the Quintillion heiress is."

"You have? That's really terrific, Ben! Our client'll be darned pleased," said Molly, giving a pleased laugh. "She can use something to cheer her up after the murder of poor Batsford and all."

"Police have any leads on his murder?"

"Nothing yet, no. But tell me about the—"

"Okay, the embryo was implanted twenty-three years ago by an outfit called Baby, Inc. The surrogate mother was—"

"Twenty-three years ago? Where the dickens was the darn thing for several decades?"

"All the startling details you'll find in the report I hope eventually to get around to writing," he assured her. "For now, the resultant girl child was adopted by a Mr. and Mrs. José S. Tempestada of the planet Esmeralda in our very own Barnum System. They christened their new daughter Timmozina."

"Great, then all we have to do next is track down this Timmozina Tempestada, explain to her that she's the long-lost heiress to an immense industrial fortune and—"

"I already know where she is."

"You do? Gee, that's a great bit of detective work. See, Snif, he isn't the lamebrain you keep saying."

"The jury is still out on that, sis."

"Go on, Ben. However did you—"

"Nowadays the young lady uses the professional name of Timmy Tempest. She's a reporter at large for *Galactic Variety,*" he said. "I've bumped into her during several investigations lately. She's not especially lovable, but she is somewhere on this very planet at the moment."

"Most of the Quintillions are sourpusses or worse, so the poor kid can't very well be expected to overcome her genetic inher—"

"I'm heading back to where you are, Molly. From there I'll find out exactly where she is," he said.

"Shouldn't take me more than a day to locate Timmy. So there's really no need for you to—"

"No, I'm still going to Cosmo's." Molly nodded her head in a mind-made-up way. "This Dr. Jenga knows something, something that she and other people think is important. If I don't find out what this is all about—well, it leaves a loose end in the case. Loose ends can foul up a case, even lead to trouble for us."

Jolson considered that. "Yeah, okay. But, Molly, be damn careful while you're up there at Cosmo's."

"She'll have me along," reminded the dog from beyond phonescreen range. "With me watching over her, she'll be perfectly safe. I personally guarantee it."

"Take care anyway," said Jolson and hung up.

CHAPTER 18

There was a small leak in the vast plaz dome that sheltered the Perpetual Flea Market. Melted snow was dripping down on the snerg-kabob vendor's cart next to the spot where Jolson, still himself, was waiting. The warm drops of water hit the bent ratman's grill, producing steamy sizzles.

"Jinxed," the ratman muttered, putting his narrow shoulder to his wheeled cart and attempting to nudge it to the left. "This location is, as often I've told you, Vera, jinxed and cursed."

His mousewoman wife was complacently munching on a candied melon on a stick. "It's a prime spot, Jerry. What's at fault, as usual, is your business acumen."

"Lend me a hand moving this thing, will you? So we can get a few feet away from this doomed location. My business sense, by the way, is top-notch."

"I suppose," observed Vera, not budging, "it was an example of your top-notch business sense that got us booked for one solid week at that Interplanetary Vegetarian Con last month."

"I converted a few of those fanatics, didn't I? Got them to try a bit of snerg."

"Three." She held up three furry fingers of her left hand. "Not what you'd call a mass conversion."

Jerry, grunting and chittering, managed to get the snerg-kabob cart to roll a few inches.

"Here now, mate," rumbled the burly bearman behind the table of secondhand dolls next to the cart. "You're on the brink of encroaching on me space."

Giving out an exasperated sigh, the ratman pointed up at the distant ceiling. "I suppose it's my fault and not an act of God that's making the roof leak? I suppose—"

"Now there, matey, you've brought up a most interesting point." The bearman rubbed his paws together. "It's what I refer to as the question of determinism versus free will. In other words, are those greasy gobs of disgusting flesh getting dribbled on because of your preordained fate or—"

"Ar, I've got no time for eggheaded debate." The rat vendor gave his cart a powerful shove. It rolled clear of the dripping, smacked into the big bearman's table of dolls.

"Have a care, mate. You're liable to—"

"Mama! Mama!"

"Papa! Papa!"

"Mama!"

Several of the supine dolls started crying.

Snorting, the bear vendor said, "Now you've gone and caused all the Little Otto dolls to wet their diapers."

"I suggested the flea market as a meeting place because I knew you'd enjoy the panorama of life it offers," said Facts-on-File, taking hold of Jolson's arm. "Let's stroll through the aisles and pretend to be eying the wonders on display. As a matter of fact, I promised the missus I'd pick her up a singing corn popper for our tenth wedding anniversary."

"I thought corn poppers were for the fifteenth anniversary."

"Hold on to that sense of humor, Jolson. It'll serve you well in your difficult career." Facts was wearing a maroon greatcoat, a neon-trimmed groutskin cap and a yellow glotie. A drop of water fell from above, hit his hat and caused a sputtering puff sound.

"What about Timmy Tempest?"

Leading Jolson along an aisle past a table piled high with used stunguns, a vendor of loaves of whole wheat bread baked in obscene shapes, and a heavyset catwoman hawking whistling coat buttons, the green informer said, "You sure are fond of skinny broads, aren't you? Molly Briggs is cute, but in the bongo department she—"

"Timmy. Her present whereabouts."

"Forty-five hundred trubux," replied Facts, pausing to inhale at a spudnut wagon.

Jolson eased out a wallet, extracted four blue-and-gold thousands and a red-and-white five hundred. "Continue," he requested, passing over the cash.

Facts-on-File folded and pocketed it swiftly. "Sir, are these donuts right here topped with coconut?" he asked of the pandaman leaning against the wagon.

The vendor cupped a paw to his ear. "How's that?"

"Is this white stuff coconut?"

"How's that?"

"I'm allergic to coconut," yelled Facts.

The donut vendor hit himself a few times in his shaggy right ear with his paw. "I thought so," he said.

"That'll teach me to buy a hearing aid at a flea market. Now then, attempt your query once again."

"Coconut."

"That's better, I'm getting you loud and clear. Although 'coconut,' you'll pardon my saying, isn't exactly a question—"

"C'mon." Jolson tugged Facts away from the donuts. "Tell me where I can find Timmy Tempest."

"She's even skinnier than Molly." He jerked a green thumb in the direction of the distant ceiling. "Timmy Tempest is up at Cosmo's."

"Doing what?"

"The lass works, as perhaps you know, for *Galactic Variety.* She embarked this very morning, via shuttle, for that fun-filled satellite," answered the information siphoner. "Timmy's scheduled to cover Studs Gunny's opening tonight at the Tropix Room at Cosmo's."

Jolson nodded. "Any notions as to who or what Cosmo himself is?"

The green man shuddered, turned away and began examining a display rack of animated neckties. "That sort of question I don't answer, for reasons of health."

"Organized crime, is he?"

"That or worse. Say, here's an interesting tie," he said, plucking a tie free of its perch. "Shows a tiny motion picture of a well-structured lady dancer named Little Egypt. Look, she's just removed her—"

"Okay, no further questions about Cosmo."

"Whatever you do," advised Facts in a lowered voice, "don't cross any of the guys who run that joint."

"I strive never to cross anybody."

CHAPTER 19

The bleached-blond catman across the shuttle aisle from Jolson clasped his nose, winced and exclaimed, "P.U. What a stench."

"Wellsir now, cousin," said Jolson amiably, "this is a darn good example of democracy in action. What I mean to say is, all us folks aboard this little shuttle bound for Cosmo's voted on what scent we wanted to have come wafting out of the aircirc system. Darned if Pine and Old Leather didn't win out."

Raising one blond eyebrow, the catman said, "I would've guessed that you voted for Bananas."

Chuckling, Jolson smacked himself on the knee with a shaggy paw. "Darned if that isn't just exactly what I did, being a gorillaman," he admitted. "Thing is, I didn't figure my favorite odor would win out, and so I was prepared to put up with what the majority of voters wanted."

"You sound like a politician."

"That's because I am, cousin," replied Jolson, who was now a husky gorillaman clad in a three-piece sky-blue bizsuit. "The name is Kissin' Jim O'Horn. I'm in the midst of running for the office of first selectman for the Affiliated Satellites and Space Colonies Orbiting Murdstone."

Nose wrinkling, the blond catman said, "Yes, I believe I've heard of you."

That was gratifying, since until an hour ago no such person as Kissin' Jim O'Horn existed in the universe. "That's gratifying, your hearing of me," he said across the aisle. "Not being affiliated with a major political party can be one heck of a handi—"

"Do you gazebos intend to gabble for the entire length of this trip?" A thin, crimson-feathered birdwoman of sixty was glaring back over her narrow shoulder at them.

"Oh, be still, you dreadful old biddy." The catman drew a pink neosilk handkerchief out of his jacket pocket and dabbed at his nose.

Jolson smiled a cordial gorilla smile at the birdwoman. "My name's Kissin' Jim O'Horn," he informed her. "Remember that when next you step into your neighborhood polling place to cast your—"

"Galloping goobers, I most certainly don't live on this blighted planet," she informed him. "I'm a citizen of Barnum, only out here on this sinkhole to give people the opportunity to hire some of my clients."

"You're in show business, are you?"

"My name is Sophie Blummer."

Jolson had never heard of her. "Of course." He rose from his seat, went thumping down the aisle in her direction. "Let me tell you how I may be able to throw some work your way." He settled into the seat beside the birdwoman, glancing casually at the two people seated across the shuttle aisle. "Of course I'm assuming you deal in *live* talent and not these second-rate android sims that are being foisted off on—"

"Climb back in your tree," suggested the lovely blonde woman opposite.

"Actually, ma'am," said Jolson, turning to smile at Betty Lou Quintillion and her companion, Cousin Rudy, "gorillas don't live in trees. And gorillamen, who superficially resemble them, don't either. So your little gibe is—"

"I can tell anybody I want to to climb a tree," Batsford's widow informed him. "Or to take a flying leap at the rolling hole in a coconut spudnut. Or to bob up and—"

"Leave the poor simp alone," drawled Rudy Quintillion, his blond head sinking further into his shoulders. "You'll have to forgive her, sir. She's in mourning and that—"

"Why, sure," said Jolson, snapping furry fingers. "I recognize you now—Mrs. Betty Lou Quintillion of the smart set. Your late hubby was just recently slain in what the media is calling—"

"Go piss up a rope. Even gorillas must be able to do that."

Rudy leaned around the blonde widow. "She's suffering from grief and from a night spent with her pretty noggin inside a brainstim—"

"Cork it, Rudy. There's really no need to confide our intimate family secrets to this hair ball."

"Ma'am, I'm Kissin' Jim O'Horn, a politician of some note. Annoying you is the furthest thing from—"

"How'd you like to kiss my rosy red—"

"Betty Lou, quit heckling," suggested the languid

Rudy, tapping her on the arm. "If you act in this fashion when we meet with Cousin Destry up on Cosmo's, he's liable to smack you silly."

"Destry can take a long walk on a short pier."

The birdwoman gave Jolson an impatient nudge. "If you're about finished hobnobbing with café society, Kissin' Jim, suppose we get down to business."

"Forgive me, ma'am." He seemingly returned his attention to her. "What I have in mind is hiring a few personable performers to travel with me while I stump the satellites in search of votes."

Bending, the feathery talent agent picked a snergskin briefcase off the floor. "I happen to represent chiefly wrestlers," she explained. "But there's no reason why a wrestler won't draw a crowd for you." Resting the case across her narrow lap, she flipped it open. "Let me show you some tri-op shots of my better talent. Here's a fellow who's very aware politically. He wrestles under the name of Rotten Rumford and . . ."

Jolson settled into his seat and feigned attention for the rest of the short shuttle trip.

CHAPTER 20

The incredibly beautiful brunette was wearing an emerald green two-piece sinsilk bathing suit. A sash draped over her shoulder and between her breasts proclaimed her *Miss Hellquad.* Smiling, she dropped Jolson's matching carpet bags on the floor of the rustic lodge. "Simulated lake, whispering pines," she announced, gesturing at the wide glaz viewindow. "Comes with the digs. All part of the famous Cosmo's service."

"A most awesome view it is, dear lady."

Miss Hellquad shut her eyes, made a low whirring noise. "Since you're registered on the first-class tourist plan, Mr. Kissin' Jim O'Horn," she said, eyes popping open, "you're allowed to fondle me and no more. Were you to pay the extra thousand trubux per day necessary to elevate you to deluxe first-class tourist, then it'd be anything goes and no questions asked."

Sauntering over to the door, Jolson opened it wider. "I did get my name of Kissin' Jim due to a pronounced fondness for the ladies," he acknowledged. "However, ma'am, I never was one for dallying with machinery. You're a very charming example of the Q-Mex art, but—"

"Well, of course I'm an andy," she admitted, walking to the doorway. "You don't think you'd get to shtup the *real* Miss Hellquad for a thousand trubux extra?"

"It would cost two or three times that, I'm well aware." He nodded at the perpetually bright afternoon outside his quarters. "Now I'd like to freshen up before hitting the casinos."

"You don't even want to fondle me?"

"I have no such urge."

"Some people are that way about mechanical women." She stepped outside. "It's what they call bigotry. Well, I hope you enjoy your stay."

Shutting the door, Jolson slipped out his bug detector and went through the small lodge. There was a standard secbug in the beam-ceilinged bedroom. He used his pocket disabler gun to turn it off without alerting anyone to the fact.

Changing into a lightweight two-piece polka-dot cazsuit, Jolson eased from the lodge and ventured into the very believable looking forest that surrounded the artificial lake and masked the other lodges in this sector. Molly was registered in Lodge 27, about half a mile downhill from here.

When he was still a quarter mile from 27, a faint beeping began in his left ear. Slowing, Jolson slipped his bug detector from his pocket.

There was a small spycam mounted in a pine tree about fifty feet ahead of him. It was looking downhill.

Pulling out the disabler and changing the setting, he fired it at the cam.

Zzzzzzuuuggggg!

The spy device would now be blind to his passing.

"That damn thing seems to be watching Molly's place."

He noticed the gatorman just after he passed under the spycam tree.

A broad fellow in a flowered three-piece funsuit, leaning against the trunk of a simulated oak and gazing downhill. He held a stunrifle under his arm and hadn't noticed Jolson yet.

Jolson took out his stungun and dodged off the trail in among the trees. Slowly and carefully he worked his way downhill. A dozen yards from the gatorman he straightened, aimed the stungun and fired.

Zzzzzzzuuummmmmmm!

The guard went up on tiptoe, stiffened, hopped forward, fell over into the brush.

There was another gatorman with a stunrifle. This one was rocking in a neowicker rocker on the porch of Molly's lodge.

Jolson, smiling cordially, walked right up to him. "Howdy there, cousin," he said, keeping his right hand in his coat pocket over his stungun.

"Take a hike."

"Exactly what I am doing. Doctor's orders." Jolson rested one big foot on the lowest step of the porch. "Can't help but admire this setup. Here we are inside a satellite, yet you'd swear this was a woodland—"

"Beat it, meatball, or I'll set fire to your hairy butt."

"Oh, that reminds me." Jolson nodded back at the way he'd come. "I spied a dead gatorman over that way. Might be he's a colleague of—"

"What did you say, peckerhead?" The rocker nearly went over when the guard leaped up out of it.

Pointing with his left hand, Jolson explained, "Big green young fellow stretched out on the sward. Dead and done for, with an expression of sheer terror etched on his visage that—"

"Out of my way!" The gatorman came clomping down the neowood steps.

Jolson allowed him to take three steps across the dry grass before using his stungun.

Zzzzzzummmmmm!

He waited on the porch for a full minute. When nobody appeared, he eased inside.

Very carefully he toured the three-room lodge and disabled the three spy devices he found. By the time he'd accomplished that he knew there'd been a struggle and that Molly wasn't around.

From the bedroom closet came a faint whimpering sound.

He went over closer to the neowood door.

". . . duty . . . cut down in the prime of life . . . alas . . ." a feeble voice was reciting.

"Sniffer," realized Jolson, yanking the door open.

Glazed of eye, lying on his metallic back with all four legs stiff, the robot hound said, "Yikes."

"Used a powerful disabler on you, looks like."

". . . unhand that maiden . . ."

Glancing around, Jolson spotted one of Molly's suitcases.

He sprinted to it, shook all the lingerie and crimefighting equipment out onto the bed. Then he hauled Sniffer free of the closet, tossed him in the suitcase and slammed it.

". . . have fallen . . . oh, the shame of it . . ."

"Be quiet in there," advised Jolson. "I'm going to have to smuggle you through the woods to my place and then repair you."

Jolson came out of his crouch, wiped his paws on his trousers and stepped back from the neoleather sofa. "You ought to be shipshape now, Snif."

The robot dog remained lying on his side, motionless. "I'm okay," he said in a forlorn voice, "mechanically, technically. But in my soul it's deepest, darkest night."

"They used a disabler on you." Jolson closed his compact tool kit, dropped it away in one of the carpet bags. "There really wasn't much you could've—"

"Not much I could've done, say you? Don't be a complete ninny, Jolson . . . That is you, isn't it, Benny, under all that fuzz?"

"It is. Now tell me what happened. Where's Molly?"

Very slowly the chrome-plated hound sat up. "I have twenty-six defense mechanisms built into me, and that's not including my wicked tongue. Yet since my unbridled vanity had persuaded me to amuse Molly with a few ditties played on the spinet in the living room of our lodge, I allowed these oafs to sneak—"

"Get to the part about the oafs. Who were they?"

"An interesting trio," replied Sniffer, scratching at an ear with a hind paw. "The opening wedge was none other than an overly handsome gent named Destry Quintillion."

"Yep, I heard he'd come up here to Cosmo's."

"This viper appeared upon the stoop of our aggressively rustic abode, claiming to be there on behalf of our client," continued the dog, not meeting Jolson's eyes. "Had I not been showing off my stride piano style, I would've gone to the door and sensed two others were lurking in the shrubbery."

"And who were they?"

"A large dim-witted robot bouncer who answers to the melodious name of Thugg. And a suave tinhorn named Sam Calamity."

"Sam Calamity? He runs the whole Cosmo's operation. He's the host in the Tropix Room and the main casino, a front man for Cosmo."

"Let me recite the rest of the shameful details." Sniffer produced a shuddering sigh. "While Destry Q. distracted Moll with some fabricated flimflam about Janella's being ill, Thugg snuck in and zonked me. The big, crude pile of scrap metal has a highly effective disabler beam built into the thumb of his left hand."

"Was Molly registered under her own name?"

"Of course not. She isn't a nitwit," answered the robot dog. "And I, lest you ask, came to the lodge inside a discreet valise. No one spotted me."

"But Destry knew you and Molly were here."

"I hate to think these gumps are smarter than we."

"Who'd Molly tell about coming to Cosmo's?"

"Nobody."

"You sure?"

"She didn't wish to discuss this little jaunt with Janella Q. until after we determined what was up with Dr. Jenga."

"But she did fill our client in about what I'd found out—that the missing heiress is Timmy Tempest."

"Molly indeed did that, yes," admitted Sniffer. "I advised her to keep mum until we'd netted that scrawny little skwack, but Moll insisted on following BIDS policy and informing the client as soon as we—"

"They must've known you and Molly were working for Janella Quintillion, and they had you watched." Jolson started to pace. "Followed you up here to Cosmo's from Murdstone, made the grab. But why do they want Molly?"

"To keep her quiet until Janella Quintillion dies."

Jolson stopped still, frowning at the dog. "How do you know—"

"I was fighting against the effects of the sapping. Although I couldn't move or help poor Moll, I was able to hear and see a mite."

"You heard Destry say he's going to kill Janella?"

Shaking his glimmering head, Sniffer replied, "Not exactly. What he said, and this is a direct quote, was: 'As soon as the Tempest girl is dead, we can announce dear Janella's passing.' "

"They know about Timmy, too," said Jolson, frown deepening.

"Be nice to know how those louts came upon that tidbit of info, wouldn't it?"

Jolson started pacing again. "Any idea where they took Molly?"

"Same place they're going to take Timmy Tempest once they snatch her—the main casino. Private offices directly below the Tropix Room. All the rooms soundproofed."

Jolson paused, eyed the robot dog. "Are you recovered enough to—"

"I'm back at my usual state of near perfection, beanpole."

"I want to take another look at the floor plans of this satellite. Can you—"

"Feast your orbs on yonder wall."

A beam of white light shot from Sniffer's left eye. On the off-white neostucco wall appeared a large blowup of an architectural drawing.

"This is the main casino, huh?"

"Righto. Next we see the layout of the famed Tropix Room. Followed by the offices below."

Jolson studied the drawing for a moment, nodding to himself. "Do you still carry disguises around inside your—"

"I ain't no ex-Chameleon, but I come equipped to impersonate several basic types of nitwitted canine—you know that. What do you have in—"

"There are three people we have to get off this damn satellite—Molly, Timmy Tempest and Dr. Jenga."

"Not to mention present company."

"I want to get to Timmy first, if possible. Then I'll go after Molly and—"

"How come Moll doesn't head the list?"

"Once they get Timmy, they may kill the others. So if I can beat them to—"

"Hold the babble for a sec, bwana." The mechanical hound's eyes clicked shut. "I'm tapping into the Cosmo's appointment books to see what assignments that rainbow-topped skwiff may be covering." He whistled a bawdy tune for about a half minute, then opened his eyes and gave a satisfied giggle. "Our gawky journalistic bimb is set to interview Studs Gunny in his dressing room at the Tropix in a shade less than an hour."

"That sounds like where they'll make their move."

"Okay, Benny, we'll be partners on this escapade." Jumping to the floor, Sniffer caused a panel in his chromed side to snap open. "How's a poodle strike you?"

"Fits right in." Crouching, Jolson took the poodle costume out of the compartment and then helped Sniffer squeeze into it. "You're going to have to solo for part of this—"

"I am always soloing, dimbulb. Even when accompanied by dolts such as—"

"When we split up, you get to the private shuttle dock, Snif, where they keep the business vehicles. Commandeer us a shuttle and stand by. Soon as I—"

"Any particular color?"

"Unobtrusive. And don't grandstand. Simply futz up their secsyst, coldcock any guards and grab us a—"

"Maybe you ought to carry me, like a pet." Sniffer suddenly hopped up into Jolson's arms. "It'll help our masquerade during its initial phase and—"

"Kissin' Jim isn't the sort to haul a poodle around. Now quit clowning and pay attention. There are a few more details to work out." He set the now-furry dog back on the floor. He scowled at him for a few seconds, then shook his head.

"If it's any comfort," said Sniffer, "I feel the same way about you, sweetheart."

CHAPTER 21

In the casino area it was always night, a steamy darkness illuminated by neon and lightstrips and throbsigns. Above an immense white palace of a building, letters twenty feet high spelled out COSMO'S.

"That last was yet another example of what I mean," Jolson was saying quietly to the trailing Sniffer.

"You expect me to let some doofus snuff out his stogie on my keester?"

"When you're impersonating a poodle you don't tell a wealthy catman tourist to go crap off a bridge, Snif."

"Fortunately I don't subscribe to the Chameleon Corps code of behavior." He chuckled. "Did you note the double take that poor gink did when I told him what he—"

"This is where you turn off." Jolson nodded at the mouth of the alley they were passing. "Soon as I locate Timmy I'll—"

"Fear not. I'll glom us a shuttle with the ease and grace for which I am—"

"Begone. And don't talk to anybody else."

"To hear is to obey, tuan." Rising up on his hind

legs, Sniffer skipped once around Jolson in the manner of an overly cute trained poodle. Dropping back to all fours, he went galloping off down the alley.

A moment later he was heard remarking, "Watch where you're relieving yourself, stewbum!"

Jolson sighed, headed for the steps of the main casino.

Sam Calamity, in a black and white three-piece tuxsuit, was sitting alone at a floating white-topped table near the center of the large, crowded Tropix Room. He puffed on his kelp cigaret, ran his hand over his slick dark hair, sipped at his glass of sinbrandy, puffed again on his kelp cigaret, flicked ashes into the pot of the nearest potted palm. "That song makes me sad, Barrelhouse," he said.

Parked next to his table was a self-playing upright robot piano. "Boss, that's the national anthem of the second planet in the Trinidad System," said the white-painted piano out of the voxbox over its keyboard. "I was playing it for that party of dignitaries from—"

"I know all about the Trinidad System," said Sam Calamity sadly, puffing and then sipping. "That was where *she* betrayed me and slept with another guy."

"Aw, sorry, boss. I thought that was in the Hellquads."

"There, too."

"You really ought to try and forget that Miss Luna dame, boss. It's really cutting down on my repertoire," complained the piano. "You don't want I should play any tune that reminds you of a place where she . . . um . . . shacked up with someone other than yourself. Turns out she was awful active during your romance, and so far you've ruled out my playing about sixteen ballads, five national anthems, a marching—"

"Stow it, Barrelhouse. You're just not equipped to understand what carrying the torch is all about, pal."

Jolson, who had been sitting two tables over from the casino manager, rose to his feet. He skirted a potted palm, dodged the stuffed green monkey dangling from it and came to a halt next to the piano. "Pleased to meet you, Mr. Calamity," he said, looming over the dapper manager. "Allow me to introduce myself to you. I'm none other than Kissin' Jim O'Horn and I'm running—"

"Beat it," advised Sam Calamity.

"I do believe you'll feel differently, cousin, once you've perused this letter from Satellite Senator Buzzino."

Sam Calamity's eyes narrowed. "You one of Buzzy's boys?"

"Let us say that he's interested in my political career." He extracted the letter that Sniffer had helped him forge, handed it to the manager. "I'm most anxious to contact Studs Gunny and enlist him in my campaign. Buzzy, as you and I call him, suggested that tonight would be a good time for my—"

"He's busy getting ready for the supper show." Sam Calamity puffed, scanned the letter. "I don't know if I can fit you in to see him or . . . five hundred thousand trubux? What's this about five hundred thousand trubux?"

"That would be your share of the fees paid out to Gunny for participating in a series of vidcommercials for my campaign. I'm running for the office of—"

"Piano music sounds terrific on politspots," mentioned the piano. "Let me play you a little political medley right now to give you an idea of the sort of talent that's right under your—"

"Political medleys make me sad," reminded Sam Calamity.

"Aw, yeah, I forgot she'd run off with that alderman on Peregrine."

"She did?" He blinked at the white piano. "I was alluding to her brief, wild fling with Dictator Obrigado on Tarragon."

"Time," put in Jolson, "is on the—"

"Sure, you're right. No reason my broken heart should hold you up, Kissin' Jim." Easing an electropen from an inner jacket pocket, the casino manager scribbled a few lines across the letter. "This'll get you by the guards and into Studs's dressing room."

Jolson took the letter in his right paw, chuckling. "You've helped the cause of honest politics no end, sir," he said. "Look for your bribe in about thirty days."

The door of Studs Gunny's dressing room opened three and a half inches. A small, puffy dead-white young toadman in a burnt-orange robe squinted out into the corridor. "Wot's er ardear of bungin' on me door, toff?"

"This letter will explain everything," said Jolson, kneeing the door open wider as he held out the folded letter.

Gunny went stumbling back, bumping into the neowood chair in front of his makeup mirror and deciding to sit. "Arf a min, yer pommy twid. Yer carn't gum bargin' inter—"

"This is a perfectly respectable business deal, Studs."

Gunny kicked a pair of lace-trimmed glopanties that lay crumpled on the floor near his chair. *"Muster* Gunny ter yer, yer shaggy hung of—"

"I'm on somewhat of a tight schedule." Shutting the door by shoving his wide gorilla backside against it, Jolson drew out his stungun.

"Ar, crikey! Anuffer looner attemptin' ter arsassinite me and—"

Zzzzzzzzzzummmmmmmmmmm!

Holstering his gun, Jolson crossed to the chair and lifted the stunned shock-rock singer out of it. He tossed Gunny over his shoulder, turned and took five steps toward the closet he intended to store him in.

The closet door swung open and a lovely tanned hand holding a kilgun appeared. "I suspected that you were up to no good the moment I first saw you."

CHAPTER 22

Beautiful blonde Betty Lou Quintillion stepped forth from the closet, keeping her gem-encrusted kilgun leveled at Jolson. "When you knocked, we thought it might be Cousin Destry checking up on me, and I jumped in—"

"Should've recognized the underwear."

At the moment Batsford's widow was naked from the waist down. "I'm nearly certain, Kissin' Jim, that you're some sort of sleazy private eye," she said accusingly. "Your crude attempt to buddy up to me on the shuttle tipped your mitt. Now that Batsy is gone, the family hopes to screw me out of what's—"

"Actually, dear lady, I happen to be one of the leading spiritualists in the entire Barnum System," he informed her. "I was, I admit, trailing you. That was, however, merely so that I might deliver a message to you from the spirit world."

"You can stuff any and all messages in your old wazoo and . . . Why are you jiggling like that?"

Jolson's wide gorilla mouth had dropped open, his hair was bristling. The spasms of shivering that had taken over his body were strong enough to cause the earrings in Studs Gunny's pale white ears to jingle.

"Oog," gasped Jolson, bending some.

"Stop quivering like that or—"

"Madam . . . oog . . . Forgive me, but . . . the spirit is taking me over, trying to contact you . . ." He stopped his shaking. Straightening, he caused his face to turn into a sudden replica of that of the late Batsford Quintillion. "Here I am, Betty Lou, not even cold in the tomb and you're back fooling around with—"

"Good gravy!" She stared, gun hand dropping to her side.

Jolson tossed the shock-rock singer he was carrying right into her.

"Oof," she said, tumbling backward and dropping her weapon.

Zzzzzuummmmmmmm!

When Betty Lou hit the floor, blanketed by Gunny, she too was unconscious.

Jolson managed to get the both of them stuffed into the closet. He then adopted the persona of Studs Gunny, dressed himself in one of the entertainer's three-piece sinsilk glosuits and sat in front of the mirror to await the arrival of Timmy Tempest.

Jolson recrossed his legs, glanced at himself again in the light-trimmed makeup mirror. He decided his spiky white hair ought to be standing about an inch higher and caused it to grow.

He drummed his puffy dead-white fingers on the makeup table, picked up a copy of Gunny's latest vidalbum, which was entitled *I'm Gonna Slit Your*

Goddamn Throat! Underneath that sat another vidcaz, this one labeled CLEANED-UP VERSION FOR YOUNGER VIEWERS and entitled *I'm Gonna Slit Your Darn Throat!*

Jolson got clear of his chair, turned toward the door. "She's nearly ten minutes overdue."

The door came flapping open. At least two dozen fat ladies came charging, tumbling, scurrying into the small dressing room. Birdwomen, toadwomen, catwomen, humans. All stout and in their middle years.

"Sorry, Studs," called a guard from the hall. "Couldn't hold them back no longer."

"Lardies, lardies," whined Jolson in his Gunny voice. "Guv me a bloomin' break, won't yer?"

They formed into a series of semicircles, facing him, smiling nervously.

A calico catwoman in a three-piece neowool travelsuit coughed into her paw and stepped clear of the first row. "We represent the Hellquad Planets Studs Gunny Fan Club," she said in a small anxious voice. "We have journeyed across the infinite reaches of space, at considerable expense, to attend your memorable performance at Cosmo's tonight. In our humble opinion you are the most lovable singer in the universe and we only wish that one of us was worthy of being your wife or sweetheart, or even, for that matter, the doormat on which your wipe your adorable little feet or even the spittoon into which you—"

"Gorsh," cut in Jolson, making shooing motions with both puffy white hands, "I'm right flattered, that I am, m'dears. Yet now I mufst request that yer take a—"

"The scroll, Grace," whispered several of the fat ladies.

"We have brought a scroll to present you as a token of—"

"INTRODUCING MISS TIMMY TEMPEST," drifted in from the corridor, along with the sound of scuffling and then running.

Ducking, Jolson started elbowing his way through his fans. "Wait ride here, lardies," he told them. "Soon's I run me errand, why, we'll have us a narse chat about your bloody scroll."

The fans giggled, murmured, sighed as he worked his way through them and out of the room.

By the time he got free to the corridor, there was no one there. Not even the guard.

Jolson dodged around another turning in the pale yellow corridor. He slowed, stopped and knelt to pick up a fallen neogold electropen from the ribbed flooring. It had TT engraved on its side.

"Something else that fell from her purse." He straightened, continued scouting the long hall.

"INTRODUCING MISS TIMMY TEMPEST, REPORTER AT LARGE FOR *GALACTIC VARIETY!*"

The talking bizcard was behind the next door on his right.

"Will youse, for cripesakes, shut that damn thing up."

"I'm trying, Thugg, but every time it falls out of the skirt's purse it starts in to—"

"Gimme that!"

Karunch! Karack!

"You doof, that card set me back—"

"I advise youse to shut your yap, sister."

Jolson knocked on the neometal door, which had PANTRY 3 glolettered on it.

"I bet that's some minions of the law. You dinks are going to get in a real jam for—"

"I don't like slapping dames in da kisser, on account of dese metal mitts of mine. But unless you—"

"Will yer open up?" whined Jolson, knocking again. About thirty-five seconds elapsed before a thickset ratman in checkered cap and plaid coat opened the door. "Take a hike, cream puff."

"Not bloody likely." Pushing him aside, Jolson went into the storeroom. "Look here now, yer fellers. I harpen ter be the bloody star of this whole shebang and when I set up an interview with a quiff, I don't—"

"Youse better scram out of here, Mr. Gunny." Thugg was near seven feet high and broad-chested. He wore the jacket of a tuxsuit on his coppery body and a licorice-hued plaz derby on his bucket head.

"Was this your notion, Gunny?" inquired the rainbow-haired Timmy, who was sitting on a large crate labelled PURPLE SPINACH.

A large apeman cradling a stunrifle stood near her.

"Lardy, it's me polercy never to turn down an interview." Jolson elbowed the door shut, crossed to the large crate.

There were cases of off-planet produce stacked all around the room—pink cabbage from Barnum, green bananas from Esmeralda, blue beans from Peregrine, etc.

Smiling, Jolson perched on the crate next to the

angry young woman. "We'll harv the interview right yere in—"

"Listen, youse," growled Thugg, tilting his derby to a more ominous angle with one large metal hand. "We got orders to hold dis quail here until . . . well, until certain important bozos get here."

"While we're waiting we can—"

"This is a security emergency," warned a dangling voxbox near the ceiling. "This is a security emergency. All special guards report to Studs Gunny's dressing room. Members of the Hellquad Planets Studs Gunny Fan Club, while rummaging for souvenirs, have found his stunned body in a closet in—"

"Time to extemporize." Jolson executed a deft backwards flip off the case.

By the time he hit the floor he had his stungun in his right hand and a disabler in his left.

Zzzzzzzummmmmmmmm!

Zzzzzziittttzzzzz!

Zzzzzzzzummmmmmmm!

Timmy clapped her hands together, watching the ratman fall over, the apeman sink down and Thugg topple backwards against a stack of neowood crates packed with shredded wheat from Earth. "Not bad for a gink who's supposed to be out cold in a closet."

He urged her off the crate and then pried off the lid with a tool built into the handle of the disabler. "Listen, Timmy, these goons were holding you for someone who intends, I'm near certain, to do you in. We have to get—"

"What happened to your repulsive accent?"

"Just an affectation. Climb inside this box and—"

"What kind of dim-witted dink do you take me—"

Zzzzzzummmmmmm!

After shaking his head, Jolson picked up the unconscious rainbow-haired reporter and arranged her in the crate atop the purple spinach.

"I've got to get back to the ceramics business," he told himself while fastening the lid back on.

Jolson adjusted his checkered cap, hunched his shoulders and pushed the hand-truck through the crowd of security people and fat ladies gathered outside the doorway of Studs Gunny's dressing room. "Coming through," he said, guiding the produce crate in and out among the bystanders.

The calico catwoman was leaning against the corridor wall. "Oh, my gracious, suppose he's dead," she said, sniffling and dabbing at her eyes with a polka-dot plyochief.

"He's breathing, Grace honey. That's always a good sign," consoled a plump toadwoman. "And as soon as he comes around, we'll present him the scroll."

"They'll surely cancel tonight's shows. That means we'll have to stay another night at Cosmo's at these outrageous rates."

Jolson, who was now impersonating the ratman he'd left stunned back in the storeroom, was nearly clear of the area when a large heavy hand grabbed his shoulder. Halting, Jolson turned.

"Where the dickens are you going, Beano?" asked a large gatorman guard.

"Don't ask me." Jolson shrugged and his plaid overcoat rose and fell.

"We could use a hand with this—"

"Naw, I got to get this load of stuff to the shuttle docks."

"Purple spinach? What's so important about—"

"Don't be a dummy." Jolson winked. "What's written on the outside of a crate don't always tell you what's inside. Get me?"

The gatorman pondered. "Hey, sure," he said after a few seconds, "I get your drift. You mean it could be . . . oh, say, illegal guns or illicit drugs or—"

"Or even a kidnapped dame, sure. But let's quit flapping our choppers about it here in public. Lemme get on with this job, pal."

"Sure thing, Beano. Did you hear some lug stunned the—"

"I heard, I heard." He started the crate rolling again.

When he got down to the corridor leading to the private shuttle dock, he encountered a toadman sitting on a stool with a stunrifle across his knees. The guard was slumped back against the pale green wall, unconscious.

Nodding, Jolson continued on.

Tappity tap tap! Tap tap tappity!

A loud metallic tapping was coming from up ahead.

Jolson started using one hand on the truck, eased his other inside the overcoat and toward the stungun.

Tap tap tap tappity tap!

He stopped at the door to the docking area, took a careful look through the plaz porthole.

"C'mon in, slim." The door swung inward to reveal Sniffer tapdancing on a stretch of metal flooring between docked shuttles designated *Cosmo's I* and *Cosmo's II.*

Jolson rolled the crate in, avoiding the unconscious dogman guard who slumbered near the tail of *Cosmo's II,* and halted near the dancing dog. "Quit that," he suggested.

Dropping to all fours, Sniffer said, "I've taken over *Cosmo's I.* The appointments are niftier, there's a larger hot tub. So wheel Miss Tempest on over."

"How'd you know I had her in the crate?"

"You set forth to fetch her. You returned with a case and I assume she's within," answered the dog. "I have faith in you, mostly because this part of the caper is so simple that even a shrab such as you can—"

"Are you capable of loading this crate into—"

"Piece of cake." A greenish beam of light went zipping from the robot's right eye.

The beam hit the crate containing the stunned Timmy Tempest. The crate rose free of the hand truck to go floating toward the open cargo hatch of the borrowed shuttle.

"Stay here and amuse yourself quietly," said Jolson. "I'll be back soon as I can."

"It's the showbiz atmosphere hereabouts that sets my feet to tapping."

Jolson left him.

CHAPTER 23

Jolson scurried along a corridor, stopped in front of a door marked SAM CALAMITY/MANAGER. He bonked the silvery neometal door with a paw.

"What is it?" inquired Calamity's voice out of the voxbox in the door.

"Boss, I got to see you," said Jolson in an agitated ratman voice.

"You're supposed to be watching that reporter dame."

"Something came up," he told the door. "It has to do with another dame, boss."

"I'm busy just now, Beano."

"This lady's name is Miss Luna and—"

"Haven't I told you bozos never to mention her name around me?"

"I didn't mention it, boss, she did."

"You mean Luna's here?"

The door came whispering open.

Jolson dashed across the threshold, right hand deep in the pocket of his plaid overcoat. "She's up in the Tropix Room right now and—"

"Damn, I was just up there mys—"

"I know. Barrelhouse told me you come down here to your office. So I—"

"Luna, huh?" Calamity stroked the artificial red carnation that decorated his lapel. "Yeah, I always had a hunch that dame would be coming back someday."

Nodding, Jolson moved closer to the manager's big ivory desk. "She says her boyfriend tossed her out . . . No, wait. It was boyfriends, plural. Her boyfriends on Esmeralda give her the bum's rush because she'd been fooling around with a visiting airhockey team from Jupiter and—"

"The same old Luna," sighed Calamity. "Well, go up and get her, Beano. I want to—"

"There's something else we have to discuss, Sam." Leaning over the desk, he brought his right hand out of the coat pocket. It held the compact black kilgun that had come with the borrowed coat.

"What in the hell are you—"

"Where's Molly Briggs?" He pointed the kilgun at Calamity's sleek head.

"Beano, I got to warn you that this sort of behavior is going to have a bad effect on your next salary review. Pal, when you pull a roscoe on Sam Calamity, you are asking for—"

"I'm asking you to tell me where you've got Molly Briggs." He poked the barrel of the black gun into Calamity's chin.

"You already know that."

"Tell me nonetheless."

"She's down in Proproom 5, on the next level." His eyes narrowed.

"What about Dr. Jenga?"

"She's there, too."

Jolson took a step backward. "I appreciate your assistance, Sam."

Calamity touched at the carnation again. "I suppose the business about Luna was all bunk."

"It was." He drew out his stungun with his free hand.

Zzzzzzzzummmmmmmmmm!

The door of Sam Calamity's office closed behind him. Jolson took five steps along the corridor and was confronted by an approaching piano.

"How's the boss doing?" asked Barrelhouse. "I decided to roll down here and find out why you were so anxious to see him."

Jolson shifted uneasily on his sneakered feet, coughed, leaned an elbow atop the white upright. "It was a sort of personal matter," he confided. "See, my ladyfriend Doris Dinkins back home on—"

"What are you trying to pull, Beano? Everybody on Cosmo's knows you're as gay as a three-trubux fruitcake."

Coughing again, Jolson said, "Well, actually, I was just asking for an advance against my salary."

"You just did that a week back."

Jolson gave a little snickering laugh and started slappng the pockets of his overcoat. "Okay, okay, Barrel," he said. "I guess I'll have to come clean and show you the real reason for my visiting Sam. Let me just find the thing and show you."

"This had better be—"

Zzzzzzzitttttzzzzzz!

Jolson had produced a disabler, fired it at the robot piano.

Barrelhouse played a few bars of honky-tonk blues, made several varied grinding sounds within and then was silent and still.

Putting the disabler away, Jolson continued on his way.

Down in front of Proproom 5, a spotted dogman guard was sitting cross-legged on a green prayer mat. A blasterifle sat on the mat next to his right thigh. "You ought to try Mercantile Transmeditation, Beano," he said beatifically. "It's changed my life."

"For the better?"

"Can't you see how much calmer I am, how much more vibrant and aware of the possibilities of existence?"

"Hard to tell when you're sitting down. Anyhow, pal, Sam Calamity sent me to see the Briggs quiff and find out if—"

"All you got to do to practice Mercantile Transmeditation is send a hundred trubux a week to Mother Trixie out in the Hellquads. Then you squat down an hour each day and contemplate all that you want to get out of your brief life and—"

"It's urgent I see this skirt."

"Sure, go on in. Door ain't locked," said the amiable guard. "But, really, Beano, you ought to try—"

"Soon as I see this dame we'll transmeditate together." He pushed opened the proproom door and entered.

The room was large, high-ceilinged and crowded

with props, costumes and scenery from former Tropix Room productions. There were rows of palm trees, piles of spangles and baubles, a stiff silent line of naked android dancing girls. Jolson worked his way around scatters of huge plaz steamer trunks and a sprawl of broken ventriloquist dummies. In a small clearing he came upon the furnishings of a parlor—sofa, coffee table, lamp and oval thermorug. Molly was slumped on the flowered sofa, hands tied in front of her and a strip of black plazband over her mouth.

After glancing around, he went over to her. "Any guards in here?" he whispered as he yanked the gag free.

"Ouch," she said, spitting sedately. "No, only outside." She scanned his ratman face. "I assume it's you, Ben, but could you, you know, identify yourself so I can be absolutely—"

"It's me." He let his face return briefly to its true form. "How about Dr. Jenga?" He worked at untying Molly.

"She's over yonder on that trampoline. I noticed her when they dragged me in here."

"Obviously you two haven't had a chance to chat."

"Couldn't have even if I wasn't muffled. She looks to have been stungunned." Molly swayed slightly as she stood. "Being tied up for a while makes you woozy. At least it does me."

He slipped an arm around her shoulders. "I'll gather up the doctor and we'll take our leave."

"Ben, we're going to have to locate Timmy Tempest. I overheard them talking and she's up here on Cosmo's and they intend to—"

"I've already retrieved Timmy from them and got her stored in a safe place. Soon as—"

"Are you telling me you rescued that frazzle-headed scatterbrain before you came hunting for me?" Molly pulled away from him. "I guess all your prior expressions of fondess for me were just so much—"

"Here we have positive proof of the folly of socializing with the boss's daughter." Jolson made his way over to the trampoline that held the unconscious Q-Mex technician. "You're letting personal stuff get in the way of—"

"Ben, I've never insisted that you rescue me before some little chit of a reporter. What I mean is, after all, you have been rendezvousing with Timmy Tempest all over the universe for months and months. Myself, the one time I saw her, while you and I were hunting for Starpirate's brain, I wasn't all that impressed. But then, some men like girls with boyish figures. Especially, I suppose, if those girls are long-lost heiresses to a multibillion-trudollar fortune and—"

"That's sufficient."

Dr. Jenga was a green-skinned woman of fifty some years, wearing a two-piece crimson cazsuit. She was overweight, but Jolson managed to get her off the trampoline and onto his shoulder.

Jolson said, "Pay attention now, Molly. I figured that once they had Timmy, they might decide to get rid of you. So I made sure I reached her first. Okay? Now, we have to get ourselves past a spiritually awakened guard outside that door and then—"

"You're not conning me, Ben? You really were concerned that I might—"

"We'll discuss all the details and manifestations of this case at a later—"

"I'd much prefer to hear the details now, Jolson." From behind a nearby palm tree stepped plump, blond Rudy Quintillion. He was holding a silver kilgun in each hand. "And so would Cosmo."

CHAPTER 24

Cosmo's office, which had one-way seethru glaz walls, offered an impressive view of the planet Murdstone far below. Across the large room a highback plaz swivelchair was turned to face a wall.

Jolson, still hefting the plump Dr. Jenga, entered the office first. Next came Molly, followed by two-gunned Cousin Rudy.

"Awfully nice to have you drop in, Jolson, Miss Briggs," drawled a slightly nasal voice from the chair. "One encounters so few first-rate people aboard a place such as this."

Jolson deposited the unconscious doctor on a floating lucite couch. "What say we have a brief brilliant chat and then take our leave of—"

"You got Timmy Tempest away from me." The chair turned around. Sitting in it was a computer terminal, its display screen an angry red at the moment. "She is no longer on the satellite, and until—"

"Gee, I pictured Cosmo much differently," observed Molly.

"Please don't interrupt, Miss Briggs," warned

Cosmo. "Now then, Jolson, allow me to explain my—"

"How'd you know I had retrieved Molly and—"

"Sam Calamity's skull has a monitor bug planted in it." The screen was growing a deeper red. "Please, dear fellow, don't keep interrupt—"

"It's a habit. Molly and I are usually—"

"Yes, we interrupt each other all the time. I suppose, you know, it does sound sort of odd to someone who—"

"If she continues babbling, Rudy, stun her."

"Give the kid a break, Coz." Rudy settled into a tin slingchair, keeping his kilguns aimed at them.

"Where's Cousin Destry?" Jolson asked him.

"About and around, hunting for dear Timmy mostly."

"Jolson, I'd prefer to use simple mindwipes on you and Miss Briggs and the doctor, causing you to forget only what you know about the Quintillion heiress and who she is," said Cosmo, his screen turning to a chill green. "That will happen, dear fellow, if you cooperate and tell me what you've done with Miss Tempest. If I have to persuade you to—"

"It's heartwarming to see a mechanism so involved in the affairs of the Quintillion clan. Or at least a certain portion of it."

"If I have to persuade you, I'll start killing you one by one," explained the terminal. "Miss Briggs first, Dr. Jenga next and you, dear fellow, last."

"Not a very efficient way of doing things."

Rudy Quintillion said, "Yes, you're really much too fond of these little games, Coz. Instead of either bargaining or threatening, why not use a truthdisc? They're highly effective and—"

"I prefer bargaining and threatening." Cosmo's display screen was scarlet again. "Much more interesting than dull, conventional gadgetry. Well, Jolson, are you going to provide the information?"

"Okay, let me explain what I think's happened." He moved closer to the seated terminal. "I turned Timmy over to an associate of mine. He in turn, and this is only a guess on my part, has apparently succeeded in spiriting her completely off Cosmo's. BIDS operatives are like that; each can work as a sort of lone wolf when the—"

"Your associate happens to be a robot mutt," said the impatient computer. "I doubt, dear fellow, that he could post a faxgram, let alone—"

"Sniffer's very bright," put in Molly. "Which he ought to be, considering the price I had to pay for him. He really can do some exceptional . . . Oops, sorry. I didn't mean to interrupt again."

Jolson had his left hand hanging by his side, close to the pocket that held the disabler. "By this time, Cosmo, Timmy is no doubt safe on Murdstone and in the hands of trustworthy law officers," he said. "You aren't going to get hold of her, so—"

Very loud piano music suddenly commenced on the other side of the office doors. It was a Venusian calypso tune that had been popular about the time Jolson had entered the Chameleon Corps academy.

Both wide glaz doors suddenly melted away to nothing and Barrelhouse came rolling in.

Taking advantage of the diversion, Jolson yanked out the disabler. Molly went for her thigh holster.

Cousin Rudy started to untangle himself from the chair, but the rampaging white upright hit him, flipping him across the room and into one of the glaz walls.

Zzzzzzummmmmmmmm!

The beam of Molly's drawn stungun caught Rudy Quintillion in midair. For an instant he formed a floating X, then hit the floor unconscious.

Zzzzzzittttttzzzzz!

Jolson had fired at the terminal, throwing himself to the left as he did. That enabled him to dodge the beam of crackling crimson light that shot out of a rod mounted atop the terminal.

"Dear fellow . . . dear fellow," muttered the wounded Cosmo. "You've . . . you've fouled up . . . entire computer and . . ." That was all.

"Suffering shad, what a bunch of boobs I have to associate with in my line of work," commented Sniffer, who came sauntering in in the wake of Barrelhouse.

Jolson asked him, "What did you do with Timmy?"

"Once I was hep to what was afoot, I deemed it best to set the shuttle on a robot flight pattern and send the lass along to Murdstone for safekeeping," the robot hound explained. "That displayed my usual brilliance, whereas you dimbulbs have been stumbling around Cosmo's like a pair of—"

"You did make sort of an impressive entry, Snif," said Molly, holstering her gun and scratching at the back of her knee.

"I encountered this rinky-tink piano—his left hand, by the by, is no match for mine—as I wended my way here to save the bacon of all and sundry," said Sniffer. "It occurred to me he'd make an excellent diversion and it wasn't especially difficult to take over his brain."

Jolson gathered up Dr. Jenga, returned her to a position over his shoulder. "Exactly how, Snif, did you know where we were and what was going on?"

"I planted a bug in your undies earlier, slim."

Jolson nodded. "That's why you jumped up into my arms," he said. "I should've known any display of affection on your part had to be—"

"Let's retreat from here, Ben."

"Yep, right."

Molly glanced back at the now-defunct computer. "It's a darn shame we didn't get to find out who's behind Cosmo," she said, heading for the doorway. "We may never learn that."

Sniffer giggled. "Don't bet on that, Moll."

CHAPTER 25

Molly said, "You seem to have forgotten my previous remarks concerning stunting."

Sniffer said, "Looping the loop is a perfectly acceptable flying technique."

Jolson said, "Loop no more."

Making a sad noise, the robot dog said, "Alas, I still have trouble getting it through my conk how conservative my colleagues are."

Cosmo's II was flying low over this Murdstone territory, en route to the place where Sniffer had dispatched *Cosmo's I* and Timmy Tempest. There was a strong wind tonight and swirling snow.

Molly was sitting in the second row of control cabin seats, behind Jolson and the piloting robot dog. "What did you mean, Sniffer, about the identity of whoever it is that Cosmo was fronting for?"

The robot dog replied, "Whilst cooling my heels and waiting for you and beanpole to extricate yourselves from Cosmo's clutches, I used my multifaceted coco to do a little probing. Now, I don't have the rep of such an illustrious info siphoner as your chum Facts-on-File, yet I ain't bad at tapping a computer."

"You tapped Cosmo?"

"Within my resplendent exterior resides a dupe of all sorts of secret data," the dog replied smugly. "Soon as we reclaim TT, I'll sort this garbage and reveal to all and sundry the . . . Aha, we've arrived at our destination."

Molly glanced out a plaz window as Sniffer punched out a landing pattern. "This can't be it," she remarked. "Nothing but a big sprawling cemetery down below."

"Exactly, and the last place you'd think to look for a misplaced heiress."

Their borrowed shuttle skimmed over a stretch of neon-trimmed obelisks, monuments and tombstones. Phrases such as *Rest in Peace* and *Free at Last* flashed and blinked in hues of blue, crimson and amber.

Bonk! Blong!

"Snif, I believe you sideswiped something."

"I merely knocked a luminous Saint Reptilicus from atop a glocrypt, Moll."

The large shuttle sat down on a clear stretch of snowy ground.

Bonk! Blong! Krackle!

"Three neon angels and a revolving *Rest in Peace* have bit the dust," said Sniffer. "Nothing to fret over." He unbuckled himself from the pilotseat. "We'll find the other shuttle about a quarter of a mile from here."

The night snow came swooping down at them as they disembarked.

Molly held on to Jolson's arm. He'd abandoned his ratman aspect, was himself once more. He still wore the plaid overcoat. "I don't see another shuttle," Molly said.

Sniffer's plaz nose lit up red and he pointed with it. "You have but to follow my unerring course," he said and went trotting off.

An imposing black brix tomb on their right was singing hymns and a circle of pint-sized android angels was dancing around a family crypt a bit further on.

"In loving memory of WING COMMANDER EDWIN MCPLAUT," boomed the voxbox embedded in a sudomarble obelisk.

"We have arrived," called Sniffer from up ahead in the snowy night.

A whirring sound commenced up above them.

Glancing up, Jolson reached for his stungun.

"That's right, folks! It's yet another low, low cost funeral from Madman Mandrake the Cut-rate Gravedigger!"

A skyhearse trimmed in emerald neon was hovering overhead.

"How can Madman Mandrake offer such insane prices for a full first-class funeral? One that includes a choir, a touching graveside euology, *and* not one, but *two* large and impressive floral pieces guaranteed to contain at least 40 percent real flowers?" asked a voxbox in the belly of the descending hearse.

"Step lively," urged Sniffer, waiting impatiently at the open doorway of *Cosmo's I.*

"The answer is simple. Madman Mandrake inters your loved ones using an entirely robot and android staff, thereby saving you the costs of human gravediggers, clerics and mourners." The skyhearse settled down a hundred yards from them.

Molly followed the robot dog up into the cabin of the shuttle. "Where did you leave Timmy?"

"The little lady is slumbering right over . . . Yeep!"

Jolson remained on the threshold. "Not here, huh?"

"She has to be," said the dog, sniffing at the seats and the floor. "I arranged her on this plush passenger seat just before I—"

"Timmy?" called out Molly. "Timmy, where are you?"

Jolson took a step into the cabin. "Note the floor, Molly."

She looked down. "Damp footprints on the thermo-carpet. Two sets."

Sniffer muttered. "Somebody beat us to her."

"Yep, they got here ahead of us and took her." Jolson reached over, caught Molly's hand and tugged. "We'd best withdraw."

"Why? Oh, you mean because they may've—"

"Quick." He got her outside and they went running across the chill white ground.

"Wait up," called Sniffer, leaping free of the shuttle.

"Observe how efficiently Madman Mandrake's efficient robot gravediggers are preparing the ground for the coffin," the hearse was saying.

Jolson and Molly dodged the shoveling robots. He got her and himself behind a fat, wide ebony vault and pulled her down beside him.

Kaboom! Blam!

The ground shook, sending up gusts of snow. Great jagged hunks of the shuttle went rocketing up into the night. Roaring flames blossomed and climbed up into the darkness. Chunks of angels and robots went flying. A shovel whapped into the side of the black tomb, close to Jolson's head.

"They expected us," said Molly in a small voice.

Jolson held on to her. "Apparently."

"Darn, I'm getting fuzzy in the head, Ben. I should've realized, soon as I saw that Timmy wasn't there, that they might have rigged that shuttle to explode once we walked in."

"We're a team," he reminded. "Sometimes I get a hunch, sometimes you do."

She turned, touched his cheek with her fingertips. "Well, I appreciate your—"

"Ahoy! I won't even point out that it's considered unseemly to smooch on sacred ground," said Sniffer, appearing around the edge of the vault. "Allow me, however, to announce to one and all that I have survived."

"That's nice," said Molly.

The robot dog sat on his haunches. "Where to now, folks?"

Jolson rose and helped Molly up. "We'll call on our client."

"Is that, you know, very smart?" she said, frowning. "What I mean is, I hate to drop in on poor ailing Janella Quintillion and admit we've lost her long-lost sister."

"But we haven't," said Jolson.

CHAPTER 26

Sniffer yawned, patting his mouth with his forepaw. "Sedately," he remarked.

"Beg pardon?" said Molly.

"I was searching for a word to describe how you fly this rented skycar."

The snow was growing heavier, the wind was stronger. Molly guided the vehicle carefully through the night sky toward Janella Quintillion's mansion. "You know, I'm beginning to suspect that all this trick flying stuff wasn't built into you at all," she told him. "You've been modifying yourself, Snif."

The robot dog rolled his plaz eyes innocently. "Me? Back in the testing department they dubbed me Old By-the-Book."

Molly glanced back over her shoulder. "Is she conscious?" she asked Jolson, who was returning from the rear compartment.

"I was able to revive Dr. Jenga, yes. Shoo." He stopped next to Sniffer's seat.

"This chair's taken, slim."

"Scoot."

"If only the rewards of life matched one's skills,

then I'd . . ." He trailed off into a mutter and rolled off the seat. He hit the floor with a woeful sound.

Jolson settled in beside Molly. "Dr. Jenga's still a mite groggy."

"But she was able to explain why she was so darn anxious to contact me and BIDS?"

He nodded. "Yeah."

"Well?"

"What the doctor told me she suspects pretty much confirms my own conclusion."

Molly said, "Honest to gosh, Ben, you're worse than Snif when it comes to acting smug about something you know that I don't know."

"I will tell you something I know."

"Which?"

"You just flew over our client's mansion."

"Oh, shoot." Molly scanned the dash controls and then started turning the skycar around.

"The one true pilot in the crowd," said Sniffer from where he was slumped on the floor, "maintains a discreet silence."

The frogman doctor was standing at the end of the dim corridor, his black medical bag held in both hands at crotch level. "I'm afraid it's quite impossible," he told them, "to allow anyone to see Miss Quintillion. It might jeopardize her very life."

"Is she much worse?" asked Molly.

Dr. Salt's broad green face became even grimmer. "To be perfectly honest, Miss Briggs," he answered, "I am commencing to fear that she may not last through the . . ." He broke down, began to sob. Dropping his bag, he tugged out a plyochief and wiped his tearful eyes. "Ah, please forgive me. It's just that I've been Miss Quintillion's personal physician for many years, and to realize that she's probably sinking into . . ." He sobbed again.

Jolson crouched down beside the robot dog, inquiring in a low voice, "Do you possess a stunbeam that can put somebody out for just an hour or so?"

"I do, though I've always considered that level a paltry pansy sort of—"

"Nevertheless, stand by."

"Aye, aye, bwana."

Grinning, Jolson straightened up. "You have to be in on this, too, Doctor," he said amiably to the physician. "Sure, things wouldn't have worked otherwise."

"Might I mention, Mr. Jolson, that you appear a trifle feverish," said the green doctor. "That may account for the hysterical ring to your recent—"

"Now, Snif."

Zzzzzziiiiiinnnnnnnnnnmmmmm!

The hour-strength stunbeam was a thin green one. It came flashing out of the robot dog's left eye and hit the nonplussed Dr. Salt in his wide chest.

Six and a half seconds later he was on the floor next to his black bag.

"Ben, what in the heck are you—"

"C'mon, we have to chat with our client."

Jolson paused, concentrated for a few seconds. Then he reached out to touch the opaque forcescreen door. He'd been able to recall Batsford Quintillion's fingerprints and the door vanished.

An even gaunter Janella Quintillion was seated in the same dark brown armchair. With her skeletal right hand she was holding an oxygen mask to her mouth and nose.

"If you're too sick, Miss Quintillion," said Molly, crossing very cautiously into the big dark room, "why, we could always come back in a day or—"

"That's all right, my dear," the gaunt woman said, lowering the breathing mask. "I'm most anxious to talk with you and your partner. So if—"

"Um . . . Ben isn't exactly a full partner, Miss Quintillion." Molly took a few more steps. "Someday, of course, my father and I hope Ben will graduate to a position of full-fledged—"

"What we have to discuss," cut in Jolson, taking a chair facing the older woman, "is your sister."

She used the oxygen mask again before saying, "I hope you've located her, Mr. Jolson. I'm awfully afraid I don't have the luxury of much more time."

"We've found her, yes."

"Miss Briggs explained to me that my sister is much younger than I, and has been using the unlikely name of . . . it's slipped my mind. What was it, Miss Briggs?"

"Timmy Tempest," she answered. "And when Ben says we've found her, what he actually means is—"

"Let me explain this." Jolson crossed his legs, leaned back in his black slingchair.

"Well, okay, but I don't want to give the impression that we—"

"Here's the basic plot, Miss Quintillion," said Jolson, the amiable grin returning to his face. "Several weeks ago a group of Quintillions—including Rudy and headed up by Destry—became extremely anxious to locate the missing Quintillion heiress. They'd been aware of the possibility she existed, but finding out what had happened to her didn't seem that urgent. For one thing, they'd been working on a scheme, I'd guess, to get control of all of Q-Mex away from you. If that worked out, it wouldn't matter any longer if the missing heiress were found or not. Because control of Q-Mex would've ceased to be something that was inherited."

"I am not aware, Mr. Jolson, of any such—"

"Trouble was, you fouled things up," continued Jolson. "Before Destry and his gang had assured control of Q-Mex, you died. That meant your sister, if she existed someplace, would inherit the entire setup."

Janella Quintillion again used the oxygen to aid her ragged breathing. "I'm afraid, Mr. Jolson, you aren't making much sense. Did you say I'd died?"

"Sure," he replied. "But Destry, Rudy and a sampling of your other loving kin didn't want that news to get out. They were afraid the missing heiress might hear it and come here to claim what was hers. So they cooked up a dodge and started hunting for the lady as well. To be on the safe side, they hired BIDS to help with the looking. Of course, if we found her they'd see that she died before claiming anything."

"I must ask you to leave," requested their client, gasping in air, "since all this wild talk is making me quite—"

"Ben, what the heck's come over you?"

He pointed a thumb at Janella Quintillion. "Molly, what does Q-Mex manufacture?"

"Well, chiefly, they make very lifelike android replicas of show business celebrities and . . . Oh, golly." She walked nearer the seated woman. "Do you mean we've been working for a sim, a mechanical replica of Janella Quintillion?"

"Yep. That's what Dr. Jenga suspected and wanted to warn you about. Destry and the gang grabbed her to prevent that."

"I'm truly surprised that an agency with the interplanetary reputation of BIDS," said Janella Quintillion, "would make such wild and outlandish accusations in—"

"This," said Jolson, slipping something out of the pocket of his plaid overcoat, "is a disabler, Miss Quintillion. As someone who's spent a lifetime around robots and androids, you know how it works. A good disabler can stop a mechanism, but it won't faze a living being at all."

"Naturally I'm aware of—"

Zzzzzzziitttzzzzz!

Jolson had fired his disabler at the seated figure.

"Oh, Ben." Molly brought a hand up to her mouth.

The woman in the chair stood, lurched, fell to the floor with a metallic thud.

Molly stared down at the fallen android. "Darn, it makes me mad to think we were hoodwinked into working for a machine that wasn't even—"

"Snif," said Jolson to the robot dog, "hide yourself."

"Are we going to indulge in parlor games to lighten the mood of—"

"Hide yourself and keep quiet."

"Ah, yes, I comprehend."

Shaking her head, Molly backed off from the Janella

Quintillion simulacrum. "She was dead before we ever started on this doggone case."

"Yep. Destry rushed through an andy copy to replace her until Timmy was found," he said, still reclining in the slingchair. "Or maybe they had one in the works even before Janella died. Dr. Jenga wasn't sure about that, but only that something odd was going on and that it involved a replica of Janella."

"When I informed our client who her long-lost sister was, I was really supplying Timmy's name to the people who were anxious to bump her off." She shook her head, sat on the edge of an umber-colored sofa. "What about Cosmo's?"

"It's more than likely that Destry and some of the family own that," said Jolson. "Running a resort/casino allows you to play some interesting tricks with money."

"Destry does own it," came Sniffer's voice. "I've been sorting through the info I swiped from Cosmo and have—"

"Silence," urged Jolson.

"Who," asked Molly, "killed Batsford? Was that Destry and company, too?"

"Has to've been." Jolson glanced toward the open doorway. "Batsford, for all his flaws, was relatively honest. He didn't know his aunt had died and been replaced by an android. Wanting to help her, he set out to do some digging himself into the whereabouts of the missing embryo. But Destry didn't want him poking around in that."

"Very astute, Jolson." The dark-tanned Destry Quintillion appeared on the threshold, a large ebony kilgun in his hand.

"Go get Timmy and bring her here," Jolson said to him. "Then we can go on our way."

Chuckling, Destry said, "I've got her up in Aunt's bedroom. And I don't think she'll live through the night." He came into the darkened living room. "Nor will any of you. You should've agreed to that brainwipe offer I made you up on Cosmo's. Now, unfortunately, you'll expire along with Timmy Tempest." He shuddered slightly. "God, what a dreadful damn name. Can you imagine the entire Quintillion Mechani operation being run by someone named Timmy?"

Jolson grinned. "Everybody can't be named Destry."

He was glancing around the dimlit room, frowning. "Where's that butthole dog of yours?"

"Sniffer isn't mine." Jolson stood up.

"Where is he?"

"Do it again, Snif," requested Jolson.

Zzzzziiiiiinnnnnnnmmmmmmm!

A beam of green light came shooting up from under the sprawled replica of Janella Quintillion. It slammed Destry in his side.

He had time to snarl and swing his kilgun halfway toward Jolson.

Then he fell.

CHAPTER 27

Timmy's hair was all one color now, a polite blonde. She was wearing a conservative three-piece gray skirtsuit and smiling a lot at Jolson. "You turned out to be not such a dunk after all," she said, catching his hand and leading him out of the mansion and into the glazdomed room that housed the swimming pool. It was a crisp, clear day outside.

"We have to get to the spaceport fairly soon," said Molly, following. "So there isn't a whole lot of time for a tour of—"

"Dip your finger in that water," Timmy invited Jolson. "It's heated just right, so you never get goose bumps when you hop in. Oh, and look at that gink sitting in the chair down at the deep end. Handsome, huh?"

"In an obvious way," said Jolson.

"That's Q-Mex Android Lifeguard/Model 28-61A. We manufacture and sell over six hundred thousand of those each and every year," Timmy explained. "When I saw him in one of our catalogs, I decided I ought to have one. My swimming isn't all that terrific, and he's cute. Not much of a conversationalist, but you can't have everything. Besides, I already got all sorts of dunks trying to court me, real-life ones."

"Sure, because you're rich now. You have to watch out for—"

"Hey, c'mon, Ben. I've been bumming around the universe since I was a kid," Timmy told him. "I know who's—"

"Our spaceliner is due to depart in less than—"

"Let me get down to business." Reaching into a pocket, she extracted a banxcheck and handed it back over her slim shoulder to Molly. "A little bonus. Because, hey, if it hadn't been for BIDS, and especially Ben, I'd have been defunct for sure by this time. And I never would've known I was an heiress."

"This is a very generous bonus, Miss Tempest . . . um . . . Miss Quintillion."

"I'm a multibillionaire now." She guided Jolson into a poolside plazchair. "I have a couple of deals to present."

He sat. "Go ahead."

She settled down next to him. "I really don't know if every single dumpus who was out to kill me has been rounded up. Sure, Destry and those people are in the hoosegow, but there could be others," she said, touching Jolson's arm. "What I'd like to do is hire somebody to sort of look after me, a super bodyguard. Someone I could trust to see that I stayed above the ground and could also maybe advise me about how the hell to run Q-Mex. Ben, I can offer you a salary that—"

"Whoa," he interrupted. "I already have a profession. Ceramics. These detective assignments are part-time things I allowed myself to—"

"Ceramics? That's a business for dunks. What I'm offering, Ben, is—"

"He has a contract with BIDS." Molly folded the check and put it into her shoulder bag. "He can't break it, no matter how much he may want to, Timmy."

"Oh, hell, any contract can be broken," she said. "I've already talked to six Q-Mex attorneys—two humans, one robot, two androids and one guy I'm not at all sure about—and they assure me that—"

"Makes no difference," said Ben. "I'm not for hire."

"Sure?"

"Yes."

"Okay, then how about this? I'd like to retain BIDS to handle my personal security."

Molly said, "That we can arrange. I'll phone you once we're back home on Barnum and outline the various plans. You can use a Murdstone affiliate or we can send some people out."

"But not Ben Jolson?"

"He doesn't work for BIDS full time."

Timmy looked over at Ben. "But you could get up here to Murdstone now and then, couldn't you? Just to see how I'm doing."

He got up, grinned. "Sure, I can do that, Timmy."

"After all, we have been friends, sort of."

He held out his hand. "True."

Ignoring the hand, she got up and kissed him on the cheek. "Thanks, Ben. I'm really going to enjoy being an heiress."

"Many do."

Molly cleared her throat. "We have a spaceliner to catch," she said.

* * *

Jolson surveyed his cabin. It was spacious, a three-room suite actually, and much more impressive than the one he'd had coming out to Murdstone. The walls were silver and ebony, the carpeting ivory. And there were baskets of fruit, vases of flowers and boxes of sweets cluttering up the parlor.

Shutting the door, he examined the nearest fruit basket. Under a purple apple he found a card: *To Ben with love from Timmy.*

"Money has mellowed that child." He moved two boxes of candy, a snergskin case of toiletries and two bouquets off a chair and strapped himself into it for takeoff.

"Welcome aboard the S.S. *Speedball,*" said a jovial voxbox up in the silvery ceiling. "Please attach your safety gear and prepare for departure. While we're waiting you'll be listening to a musical interlude with Merle and His Magic Violin."

Eleven minutes later the spaceliner was on its way to Barnum.

Leaving the chair, Jolson began cataloguing the various gifts. All were from Timmy.

He was still counting boxes of candy when a tapping sounded on the door. "Come on in," he invited.

Molly entered. "When does the wake start?"

"Didn't she send you any bon voyage gifts?"

"A dozen yellow roses and a two-pound box of carob-covered goobers," Molly answered. "You really made an impression on her. Well, she's young and impressionable, and from her perspective you probably appear to be a dashing, heroic fellow who saved her life and paved the way for her to inherit a vast fortune."

"I am a dashing, heroic fellow," he said. "And I did save Timmy's life and pave the way for her to inherit a vast fortune."

"Now that you mention it, I guess that's so." Molly placed candy boxes and fruit baskets on the floor and sat on a glaz loveseat. "I guess I'm refusing to admit that I botched my side of the investigation and—"

"You didn't botch anything," he assured her. "Well, nothing major."

She opened a candy box. "Chocolate-covered sourbugs." Her nose wrinkled. "Never one of my favorites." She shut the box. "Have you seen Sniffer? I lost track of him just after we boarded the liner."

"He's in with the baggage."

"Isn't he going to complain about that?"

"He isn't even going to be aware of it until he awakens on Barnum."

"Did you tamper with his inner workings so that—"

"I did, yes," he admitted. "Chiefly because I didn't want to be heckled on this trip. By him or you."

"My intention in coming here to your cabin wasn't to heckle you— Say, how come your cabin is so much bigger than mine?"

"Must be Timmy's doing."

She stood. "Heck, I can see that the junior partner of an interplanetary detective agency is no match for an heiress who can give people rooms full of—"

"The other reason I incapacitated Snif," said Jolson, "was so that he wouldn't walk in on us."

"Walk in on us while we were . . . Oh, yes, I see,"

she said. "Do you really think we ought to continue our . . . um . . . romance?"

"Matter of fact, yes."

"Then you really haven't been swayed by Timmy's temptations?"

"Not much, no."

Molly crossed to the open doorway of his bedroom. "You'd better give me a hand with this."

"With what?"

"We're going to have to move all those flowers and boxes of candy off the bed," she said, "before we can use it."